S0-ARV-608

Miss Minerva
and
William Green Hill

BY

FRANCES BOYD CALHOUN

Illustrated by

ANGUS MACDONALL

The Reilly & Lee Co.

CHICAGO

Miss Minerva and William Green Hill

COPYRIGHT, MCMIX BY
THE REILLY & BRITTON CO.
ALL RIGHTS RESERVED, MADE
IN U. S. A. . . . . FORTY NINTH EDITION

CONTENTS

MISS MINERVA AND WILLIAM GREEN HILL

CHAPTER I

A SCANDALIZED VIRGIN

HE bus drove up to the gate and stopped under the electric street-light. Perched on the box by the big, black negro driver sat a little boy whose slender figure was swathed in a huge rain coat.

Miss Minerva was on the porch waiting to receive him.

"Mercy on me, child," she said, "what on earth made you ride up there? Why didn't you get inside?"

"I jest wanted to ride by Sam Lamb," replied the child as he was lifted down. "An' I see a nice fat little man name' Major ——"

"He jes' wouldn't ride inside, Miss Minerva," interrupted the driver, quickly, to pass over the blush that rose to the spinster's thin cheek at mention of the Major. "Twarn't no use fer ter try ter make him ride nowhars but jes' up by me. He jes' 'fused an' 'fused an' 'sputed an' 'sputed; he jes' tuck ter me f'om de minute he got off 'm de train an' sot eyes on me; he am one easy chile ter git 'quainted wid; so, I jes' h'isted him up by me. Here am his verlise, ma'am."

"Good-bye, Sam Lamb," said the child as the negro got back on the box and gathered up the reins. "I'll see you to-morrer."

Miss Minerva imprinted a thin, old-maid kiss on the sweet, childish mouth. "I am your Aunt Minerva," she said, as she picked up his satchel.

The little boy carelessly drew the back of his hand across his mouth.

"What are you doing?" she asked. "Are you wiping my kiss off?"

"Naw'm," he replied, "I's jest a—I's a-rubbin' it in, I reckon."

"Come in, William," and his aunt led the way through the wide hall into a big bedroom.

"Billy, ma'am," corrected her nephew.

"William," firmly repeated Miss Minerva. "You may have been called Billy on that plantation where you were allowed to run wild with the negroes, but your name is William Green Hill and I shall insist upon your being called by it."

She stooped to help him off with his coat, remarking as she did so, "What a big overcoat; it is several sizes too large for you."

"Darned if 'tain't," agreed the child promptly.

"Who taught you such a naughty word?" she asked in a horrified voice. "Don't you know it is wrong to curse?"

"You call that cussin'?" came in scornful tones from the little boy. "You don't know cussin' when you see it; you jest oughter hear ole Uncle Jimmy-Jawed Jup'ter, Aunt Cindy's husban'; he'll show you somer the pretties' cussin' you ever did hear."

"Who is Aunt Cindy?"

"She's the colored 'oman what 'tends to me ever sence me an' Wilkes Booth Lincoln's born, an' Uncle Jup'ter is her husban' an' he sho' is a stingeree on cussin'. Is yo' husban' much of a cusser?" he inquired.

A pale pink dyed Miss Minerva's thin, sallow face.

"I am not a married woman," she replied, curtly, "and I most assuredly would not permit any oaths to be used on my premises."

"Well, Uncle Jimmy-Jawed Jup'ter is jest nach'elly boun' to cuss,— he's got a repertation to keep up," said Billy.

He sat down in a chair in front of his aunt, crossed his legs and smiled confidentially up into her face.

"Hell an' damn is jest easy ev'yday words

to that nigger. I wish you could hear him
cuss on a Sunday jest one time, Aunt Minerva; he'd sho' make you open yo' eyes
an' take in yo' sign. But Aunt Cindy
don't 'low me an' Wilkes Booth Lincoln to
say nothin' 't all only jest 'darn' tell we
gits grown mens, an' puts on long pants."

"Wilkes Booth Lincoln?" questioned his
aunt.

"Ain't you never hear teller him?" asked
the child. "He's ole Aunt Blue-Gum
Tempy's Peruny Pearline's boy; an' Peruny
Pearline," he continued enthusiastically,
"she ain't no ord'nary nigger; her hair ain't
got nare kink an' she's got the grandes'
clo'es. They ain't nothin' snide 'bout her.
She got ten chillens an' ev'y single one of
'em's got a diff'unt pappy, she been married
so much. They do say she got Injun blood
in her, too."

Miss Minerva, who had been standing

prim, erect, and stiff, fell limply into a convenient rocking chair, and looked closely at this orphaned nephew who had come to live with her.

She saw a beautiful, bright, attractive little face out of which big, saucy gray eyes shaded by long curling black lashes looked winningly at her; she saw a sweet, childish red mouth, a mass of short, yellow curls, and a thin but graceful little figure.

"I knows the names of aller ole Aunt Blue-Gum Tempy's Peruny Pearline's chillens," he was saying proudly: "Admiral Farragut Moses the Prophet Esquire, he's the bigges'; an' Alice Ann Maria Dan Stepan'-Go-Fetch-It, she had to nuss all the res'; she say fas' as she git th'oo nussin' one an' 'low she goin' to have a breathin' spell, here come another one an' she got to nuss it. An' the nex' is Mount Sinai Tabernicle; he name fer the church where ol' Aunt Blue-Gum

Tempy's Peruny Pearline takes her sacker-
ment; an' the nex' is First Thessalonians;
Second Thessalonians, he's dead an' gone
to the Bad Place 'cause he skunt a cat, — I
don't mean skin the cat on a actin' pole like
me an' Wilkes Booth Lincoln does — he
skunt a sho' 'nough cat what was a black cat,
what was a ole witch, an' she come back an'
ha'nt him an' he growed thinner an' thinner
an' weasler an' weasler, tell finely he wa'n't
nothin' 't all but a skel'ton, an' the Bad Man
won't 'low nobody 't all to give his parch'
tongue no water, an' he got to, ever after
amen, be toast on a pitchfork. An' Oleander
Magnolia Althea is the nex'," he continued,
enumerating Peruny Pearline's offspring on
his thin, well molded fingers; "she got the
seven-year itch; an' Gettysburg, an' Biddle-
&-Brothers-Mercantile-Co; he name fer the
sto' where ole Aunt Blue-Gum Tempy's Peruny Pearline gits credit so she can pay when

she fetches in her cotton in the fall; an'
Wilkes Booth Lincoln, him an' me's twins;
we was borned the same day only I's borned
to my mama an' he's borned to hisn an' Doctor Jenkins fetched me an' Doctor Shacklefoot fetched him. An' Decimus Ultimus,"
— the little boy triumphantly put his right
forefinger on his left little one, thus making
the tenth, — "she's the baby an' she's got the
colic an' cries loud 'nough to wake up Israel;
Wilkes Booth Lincoln say he wish the little
devil would die. Peruny Pearline firs' name
her 'Doctor Shacklefoot' 'cause he fetches
all her chillens, but the doctor he say that
ain't no name fer a girl, so he name her
Decimus Ultimus."

Miss Minerva, sober, proper, dignified, religious old maid unused to children, listened
in frozen amazement and paralyzed silence.
She decided to put the child to bed at once
that she might collect her thoughts, and lay

some plans for the rearing of this sadly neglected little orphaned nephew.

"William," she said, "it is bedtime, and
I know you must be sleepy after your long

ride on the cars. Would you like something
to eat before I put you to bed? I saved you
some supper."

"Naw 'm, I ain't hongry; the Major man
what I talk to on the train tuck me in the
dinin'-room an' gimme all I could hol'; I

jest eat an' eat tell they wa'n't a wrinkle in me," was the reply. "He axed me 'bout you, too. Is he name' Major Minerva?"

She opened a door in considerable confusion, and they entered a small, neat room adjoining.

"This is your own little room, William," said she; "you see it opens into mine. Have you a night-shirt?"

"Naw'm, I don' need no night-shirt. I jest sleeps in my unions and sometimes in my overalls."

"Well, you may sleep in your union suit to-night," said his scandalized relative, "and I'll see what I can do for you to-morrow. Can you undress yourself?"

Her small nephew wrinkled his nose, disdainfully. "Well, I reckon so," he scornfully made answer. "Me an' Wilkes Booth Lincoln been undressin' usself ever since we's born."

"I'll come in here after a while and turn off the light. Good night, William."

"Good night, Aunt Minerva," responded the little boy.

CHAPTER II

THE RABBIT'S LEFT HIND FOOT

FEW minutes later, as Miss Minerva sat rocking and thinking, the door opened and a lean, graceful, little figure, clad in a skinny, gray union suit, came hesitantly into the room.

"Ain't I a-goin' to say no prayers?" demanded a sweet, childish voice. "Aunt Cindy hear me an' Wilkes Booth Lincoln say us prayers ev'y night sence we's born."

"Why, of course you must say your prayers," said his aunt, blushing at having to be reminded of her duty by this young heathen; "kneel down here by me."

Billy looked at his aunt's bony frame and thought of Aunt Cindy's soft, fat, ample lap. A wistful look crossed his childish face as

he dropped down in front of her and laid
his head against her knee, then the bright,
beautiful little face took on an angelic expression as he closed his eyes and softly
chanted:

"'Now I lays me down to sleep,
　I prays the Lord my soul to keep,
　If I should die befo' I wake,
　I prays the Lord my soul to take.

"'Keep way f'om me hoodoo an' witch,
　Lead my paf f'om the po'-house gate,
　I pines fer the golden harps an' sich,
　Oh, Lord, I'll set an' pray an' wait.'

"Oh, Lord, bless ev'ybody; bless me an'
Aunt Cindy, an' Wilkes Booth Lincoln, an'
Aunt Blue-Gum Tempy's Peruny Pearline,
an' Uncle Jimmy-Jawed Jup'ter, an' ev'y-
body, an' Sam Lamb, an' Aunt Minerva, an'
aller Aunt Blue-Gum Tempy's Peruny Pear-

line's chillens, an' give Aunt Minerva a billy
goat or a little nanny if she'd ruther, an'
bless Major Minerva, an' make me a good

boy like Sanctified Sophy, fer Jesus' sake.
Amen."

"What is that you have tied around your

neck, William?" she asked, as the little boy rose to his feet.

"That's my rabbit foot; you won't never have no 'sease 't all an' nobody can't never conjure you if you wears a rabbit foot. This here one is the lef' hin' foot; it was ketched by a red-headed nigger with cross-eyes, in a graveyard at twelve er'clock on a Friday night, when they's a full moon. He give it to Aunt Cindy to tie 'roun' my nake when I's a baby. Ain't you got no rabbit foot?" he anxiously inquired.

"No," she answered. "I have never had one and I have never been conjured either. Give it to me, William; I can not allow you to be so superstitious," and she held out her hand.

"Please, Aunt Minerva, jest lemme wear it to-night," he pleaded. "Me an' Wilkes Booth Lincoln's been wearing us rabbit foots ever sence we's born."

"No," she said firmly; "I'll put a stop to such nonsense at once. Give it to me, William."

Billy looked at his aunt's austere countenance and lovingly fingered his charm; he opened his mouth to say something, but hesitated; slowly he untied the string around his neck and laid his treasure on her lap; then without looking up, he ran into his own little room, closing the door behind him.

Soon afterward Miss Minerva, hearing a sound like a stifled sob coming from the adjoining room, opened the door softly and looked into a sad little face with big, wide, open eyes shining with tears.

"What is the matter, William?" she coldly asked.

"I ain't never slep' by myself," he sobbed. "Wilkes Booth Lincoln always sleep on a pallet by my bed ever sence we's born an' —

an' I wants Aunt Cindy to tell me 'bout Uncle Piljerk Peter."

His aunt sat down on the bed by his side. She was not versed in the ways of childhood and could not know that the little boy wanted to pillow his head on Aunt Cindy's soft and ample bosom, that he was homesick for his black friends, the only companions he had ever known.

"I'll tell you a Bible story," she temporized. "You must not be a baby. You are not afraid, are you, William? God is always with you."

"I don' want no God," he sullenly made reply; "I wants somebody with sho' 'nough skin an' bones, an'—an' I wants to hear 'bout Uncle Piljerk Peter."

"I will tell you a Bible story," again suggested his aunt; "I will tell you about—"

"I don' want to hear no Bible story, neither," he objected; "I wants to hear

Uncle Jimmy-Jawed Jup'ter play his 'corjun an' sing:

" 'Rabbit up the gum tree, Coon is in the
      holler;
  Wake, Snake; Juney-Bug stole a half a
      dollar.' "

"I 'll sing you a hymn," said Miss Minerva patiently.

"I don' want to hear you sing no hymn," said Billy impolitely. "I wants to see Sanctified Sophy shout."

As his aunt could think of no substitute with which to tempt him in lieu of Sanctified Sophy's shouting, she remained silent.

"An' I wants Wilkes Booth Lincoln to dance a clog," persisted her nephew.

Miss Minerva still remained silent. She felt unable to cope with the situation till she had adjusted her thoughts and made her plans.

Presently Billy, looking at her shrewdly, said:

"Gimme my rabbit foot, Aunt Minerva, an' I'll go right off to sleep."

When she again looked in on him he was fast asleep, a rosy flush on his babyish, tear-stained cheek, his red lips half parted, his curly head pillowed on his arm, and close against his soft, young throat there nestled the left hind foot of a rabbit.

Miss Minerva's bedtime was half after nine o'clock, summer or winter. She had hardly varied a second in the years that had elapsed since the runaway marriage of her only relative, the young sister whose child had now come to live with her. But on the night of Billy's arrival the stern, narrow woman sat for hours in her rocking chair, her mind busy with thoughts of that pretty young sister, dead since the boy's birth.

And now the wild, reckless, dissipated

brother-in-law was dead, too, and the child
had been sent to her; to the aunt who did
not want him, who did not care for children,
who had never forgiven her sister her un-
fortunate marriage. "If he had only been a
girl," she sighed. What she believed to be
a happy thought entered her brain.

"I shall rear him," she promised herself,
"just as if he were a little girl; then he will
be both a pleasure and a comfort to me, and
a companion for my loneliness."

Miss Minerva was strictly methodical;
she worked ever by the clock, so many hours
for this, so many minutes for that. William,
she now resolved, for the first time becom-
ing really interested in him, should grow up
to be a model young man, a splendid and
wonderful piece of mechanism, a fine, practical, machine-like individual, moral, upright, religious. She was glad that he was
young; she would begin his training on the

morrow. She would teach him to sew, to sweep, to churn, to cook, and when he was older he should be educated for the ministry.

"Yes," said Miss Minerva; "I shall be very strict with him just at first, and punish him for the slightest disobedience or misdemeanor, and he will soon learn that my authority is not to be questioned."

And the little boy who had never had a restraining hand laid upon him in his short life? He slept sweetly and innocently in the next room, dreaming of the care-free existence on the plantation and of his idle, happy, companions.

CHAPTER III

THE WILLING WORKER

"GET up, William," said Miss Minerva, "and come with me to the bath-room; I have fixed your bath."

The child's sleepy eyes popped wide open at this astounding command.

"Ain't this-here Wednesday?" he asked.

"Yes; to-day is Wednesday. Hurry up or your water will get cold."

"Well, me an' Wilkes Booth Lincoln jest washed las' Sat'day. We ain't got to wash no mo' till nex' Sat'day," he argued.

"Oh, yes," said his relative; "you must bathe every day."

"Me an' Wilkes Booth Lincoln ain't never wash on a Wednesday sence we's born," he protested indignantly.

Billy's idea of a bath was taken from the severe weekly scrubbing which Aunt Cindy gave him with a hard washrag, and he felt that he'd rather die at once than have to bathe every day.

He followed his aunt dolefully to the bathroom at the end of the long back-porch of the old-fashioned, one-story house; but once in the big white tub he was delighted.

In fact, he stayed in it so long Miss Minerva had to knock on the door and tell him to hurry up and get ready for breakfast.

"Say," he yelled out to her, "I likes this-here; it's mos' as fine as Johnny's Wash Hole where me an' Wilkes Booth Lincoln goes in swimmin' ever sence we's born."

When he came into the dining-room he was a sight to gladden even a prim old maid's heart. The water had curled his hair into riotous yellow ringlets, his bright eyes gleamed, his beautiful, expressive little face shone happily, and every movement of his agile, lithe figure was grace itself.

"I sho' is hongry," he remarked, as he took his seat at the breakfast table.

Miss Minerva realized that now was the time to begin her small nephew's training; if she was ever to teach him to speak correctly she would have to begin his education at once.

"William," she said sternly, "you must not talk so much like a negro. Instead of saying 'I sho' is hongry,' you should say, 'I am very hungry.' Listen to me and try to speak more correctly.

"Don't! don't!" she screamed as he helped himself to the meat and gravy, leaving a little brown river on her fresh white table-cloth. "Wait until I ask a blessing; then I will help you to what you want."

Billy enjoyed his breakfast very much. "These muffins sho' is—" he began; catch-

ing his aunt's eye he corrected himself:
"These muffins am very good."

"These muffins are very good," said Miss
Minerva patiently.

"Did you ever eat any bobbycued rabbit?"
he asked. "Me an' Wilkes Booth Lincoln
been eatin' chitlins, an' sweet 'taters, an'
'possum, an' squirrel, an' hoe-cake, an'
Brunswick stew ever sence we's born," was
his proud announcement.

"Use your napkin," commanded she, "and
don't fill your mouth so full."

The little boy flooded his plate with syrup.

"These-here 'lasses sho' is—" he began,
but instantly remembering that he must be
more particular in his speech, he stammered
out:

"These-here sho' is—am—are a nice
messer 'lasses. I ain't never eat sech a good
bait. They sho' is—I aimed to say—these
'lasses sho' are a bird; they's 'nother sight

tastier'n sorghum, an' Aunt Cindy 'lows that sorghum sure is the very penurity of a nigger."

She did not again correct him.

"I must be very patient," she thought, "and go very slowly. I must not expect too much of him at first."

After breakfast Miss Minerva, who would not keep a servant, preferring to do her own work, tied a big cook-apron around the little boy's neck, and told him to churn while she washed the dishes. This arrangement did not suit Billy.

"Boys don't churn," he said sullenly; "me an' Wilkes Booth Lincoln don' never have to churn sence we's born; 'omans has to churn an' I ain't a-going to. Major Minerva—he ain't never churn," he began belligerently, but his relative turned an uncompromising and rather perturbed back upon him. Realizing that he was beaten, he submitted to his fate, clutched the dasher angrily, and began his weary work.

He was glad his little black friend did not witness his disgrace.

As he thought of Wilkes Booth Lincoln the big tears came into his eyes and rolled down his cheeks; he leaned way over the churn and the great glistening tears splashed right into the hole made for the dasher, and rolled into the milk.

Billy grew interested at once and laughed aloud; he puckered up his face and tried to weep again, for he wanted more tears to fall into the churn; but the tears refused to come and he couldn't squeeze another one out of his eyes.

"Aunt Minerva," he said mischievously, "I done ruint yo' buttermilk."

"What have you done?" she inquired.

"It's done ruint," he replied; "you'll hafter th'ow it away; 'tain't fitten fer nothin'. I done cried 'bout a bucketful in it."

"Why did you cry?" asked Miss Minerva calmly. "Don't you like to work?"

"Yes'm, I jes' loves to work; I wish I had time to work all the time. But it makes my belly ache to churn,—I got a awful pain right now."

"Churn on!" she commanded unsympathetically.

He grabbed the dasher and churned vigorously for one minute.

"I reckon the butter's done come," he announced, resting from his labors.

"It hasn't begun to come yet," replied the exasperated woman. "Don't waste so much time, William."

The child churned in silence for the space of two minutes, and suggested: "It's time to put hot water in it; Aunt Cindy always puts hot water in it. Lemme git some fer you."

"I never put hot water in my milk," said she, "it makes the butter puffy. Work more and talk less, William."

Again there was a brief silence, broken only by the sound of the dasher thumping against the bottom of the churn, and the rattle of the dishes.

"I sho' is tired," he presently remarked, heaving a deep sigh. "My arms is 'bout give out, Aunt Minerva. Ole Aunt Blue-Gum Tempy's Peruny Pearline see a man churn with his toes; lemme git a chair an' see if I can't churn with my toes."

"Indeed you shall not," responded his annoyed relative positively.

"Sanctified Sophy knowed a colored 'oman what had a little dog went roun' an' roun' an' churn fer her," remarked Billy after a short pause. "If you had a billy goat or a little nanny I could hitch him to the churn fer you ev'ry day."

"William," commanded his aunt, "don't say another word until you have finished your work."

"Can't I sing?" he asked.

She nodded permission as she went through the open door into the dining-room.

Returning a few minutes later she found him sitting astride the churn, using the dasher so vigorously that buttermilk was splashing in every direction, and singing in a clear, sweet voice:

"He'll feed you when you's naked,
　　The orphan stear he'll dry,
　　He'll clothe you when you's hongry
　　An' take you when you die."

Miss Minerva jerked him off with no gentle hand.

"What I done now?" asked the boy innocently. "'Tain't no harm as I can see jes' to straddle a churn."

"Go out in the front yard," commanded

his aunt, "and sit in the swing till I call you. I'll finish the work without your assistance." And, William," she called after him, "there is a very bad little boy who lives next door; I want you to have as little to do with him as possible."

A.MM.D.

CHAPTER IV

SWEETHEART AND PARTNER

ILLY was sitting quietly in the big lawn-swing when his aunt, dressed for the street, finally came through the front door.

"I am going up-town, William," she said; "I want to buy you some things that you may go with me to church Sunday. Have you ever been to Sunday school?"

"Naw 'm; but I been to pertracted meetin'," came the ready response. "I see Sanctified Sophy shout tell she tore ev'ry rag offer her back 'ceptin' a shimmy. She 's one 'oman what sho' is got 'ligion; she ain't never backslid 't all, an' she ain't never fell f'om grace but one time—"

"Stay right in the yard till I come back. Sit in the swing and don't go outside the front yard. I shan't be gone long," said Miss Minerva.

His aunt had hardly left the gate before Billy caught sight of a round, fat little face peering at him through the palings which separated Miss Minerva's yard from that of her next-door neighbor.

"Hello!" shouted Billy. "Is you the bad little boy what can't play with me?"

"What you doing in Miss Minerva's yard?" came the answering interrogation across the fence.

"I's come to live with her," replied Billy. "My mama an' papa is dead. What's yo' name?"

"I'm Jimmy Garner. How old are you? I'm most six, I am."

"Shucks, I's already six, a-going on seven. Come on, le's swing."

"Can't," said the new acquaintance; "I've runned off once to-day, and got licked."

"I ain't never got no whippin' sence me an' Wilkes Booth Lincoln's born." boasted Billy.

"Ain't you?" asked Jimmy. "I 'spec' I been whipped more 'n a million times, my mama is so pertic'lar with me. She's 'bout the pertic'larest woman ever was; she don't 'low me to leave the yard 'thout I get a whipping. I believe I will come over to see you 'bout half a minute."

Suiting the action to the word, Jimmy climbed the fence, and the two little boys were soon comfortably settled facing each other in the big lawn-swing.

"Who lives over there?" asked Billy, pointing to the house across the street.

"That's Miss Cecilia's house. That's her coming out of the front gate now."

The young lady smiled and waved her hand at them.

"Ain't she a peach?" asked Jimmy. "She's

my sweetheart and she is 'bout the swellest sweetheart they is."

"She's mine, too," promptly replied Billy, who had fallen in love at first sight. "I's a-goin' to have her fer my sweetheart too."

"Naw, she ain't yours, neither; she's mine," angrily declared the other little boy, kicking his rival's legs. "You all time talking 'bout you going to have Miss Cecilia for your sweetheart. She's promised me."

"I'll tell you what," proposed Billy; "lemme have her an' you can have Aunt Minerva."

"I wouldn't have Miss Minerva to save your life," replied Jimmy disrespectfully; "her nake ain't no bigger 'n that," making a circle of his thumb and forefinger. "Miss Cecilia, Miss Cecilia," he shrieked tantalizingly, "is my sweetheart."

"I'll betcher I have her fer a sweetheart soon as ever I see her," said Billy.

"What's your name?" asked Jimmy presently.

"Aunt Minerva says it's William Green Hill, but 'tain't—it's jest plain Billy," responded the little boy.

"Ain't God a nice, good old man," remarked Billy, after they had swung in silence for a while, with an evident desire to make talk.

"That He is," replied Jimmy, enthusiastically. "He's 'bout the forgivingest person ever was. I just couldn't get 'long a-tall 'thout Him. It don't make no differ'nce what you do or how many times you run off, all you got to do is just ask God to forgive you and tell Him you're sorry and ain't going to do so no more, that night when you say your prayers, and it's all right with God. S'posing He was one of these wants-his-own-way kind o' mans, He could make Hisself the troublesomest person ever was, and little boys couldn't do nothing a-tall. I sure think a heap of God. He ain't never give me the worst of it yet."

"I wonder what He looks like," mused Billy.

"I s'pec' He just looks like the three-headed giant in Jack the Giant-Giller," explained Jimmy, "'cause He's got three heads and one body. His heads are name' Papa, Son, and Holy Ghost, and His body is just name' plain God. Miss Cecilia 'splained it all to me and she is 'bout the splendidest 'splainer they is. She's my Sunday-school teacher."

"She's going to be my Sunday-school teacher, too," said Billy serenely.

"Yours nothing; you all time want my Sunday-school teacher."

"Jimmee!" called a voice from the interior of the house in the next yard.

"Somebody's a-callin' you," said Billy.

"That ain't nobody but mama," explained Jimmy composedly.

"Jimmee-ee!" called the voice.

"Don't make no noise," warned that little boy; "maybe she'll give up toreckly."

"You Jimmee!" his mother called again.

Jimmy made no move to leave the swing.

"I don' never have to go 'less she says 'James Lafayette Garner,' then I got to hustle," he remarked.

"Jimmy Garner!"

"She's mighty near got me," he said softly; "but maybe she'll get tired and won't call no more. She ain't plumb mad yet."

"James Garner!"

"It's coming now," said Jimmy dolefully. The two little boys sat very still and quiet.

"James Lafayette Garner!"

The younger child sprang to his feet.

"I got to get a move on now," he said; "when she calls like that she means business.

I betcher she's got a switch and a hair-brush
and a slipper in her hand right this minute.
I'll be back toreckly," he promised.

He was as good as his word, and in a very
short time he was sitting again facing Billy
in the swing.

"She just wanted to know where her em-
broid'ry scissors was," he explained. "It
don't matter what's lost in that house, I'm
always the one that's got to be 'sponsible
and all time got to go look for it."

"Did you find 'em?" asked Billy.

"Yep; I went right straight where I left
'em yeste'day. I had 'em trying to cut a piece
of wire. I stole off and went down to Sam
Lamb's house this morning and tooken breakfast with him and his old woman, Sukey,"
he boasted.

"I knows Sam Lamb," said Billy; "I rode
up on the bus with him."

"He's my partner," remarked Jimmy.

"He's mine, too," said Billy quickly.

"No, he ain't neither; you all time talking 'bout you going to have Sam Lamb for a partner. You want everything I got. You want Miss Cecilia and you want Sam Lamb. Well, you just ain't a-going to have 'em. You got to get somebody else for your partner and sweetheart."

"Well, you jest wait an' see," said Billy. "I got Major Minerva."

"Shucks, they ain't no Major name' that a-way," and Jimmy changed the subject. "Sam Lamb's sow's got seven little pigs. He lemme see 'em suck," said Sam Lamb's partner proudly. "He's got a cow, too; and she's got the worrisomest horns ever was. I believe she's a steer anyway.

"Shucks," said the country boy, contemptuously; "you do' know a steer when you see one; you can't milk no steer."

CHAPTER V

TURNING ON THE HOSE

"OOK! Ain't that a snake?" shrieked Billy, pointing to what looked to him like a big snake coiled in the yard.

"Snake, nothing!" sneered his companion; "that's a hose. You all time got to call a hose a snake. Come on, let's sprinkle," and Jimmy sprang out of the swing, jerked up the hose, and dragged it to the hydrant. "My mama don't never 'low me to sprinkle with her hose, but Miss Minerva she's so good I don' reckon she'll care," he cried mendaciously.

Billy followed, watched his companion screw the hose to the faucet, and turn the water on. There was a hissing, gurgling sound and a stream of water shot out, much to the rapture of the astonished Billy.

"Won't Aunt Minerva care?" he asked, anxiously. "Is she a real 'ligious 'oman?"

"She is the Christianest woman they is," announced the other child. "Come on, we'll sprinkle the street—and I don't want nobody to get in our way, neither."

"I wish Wilkes Booth Lincoln could see us," said Miss Minerva's nephew.

A big, fat negress, with a bundle of clothes tied in a red tablecloth on her head, came waddling down the sidewalk.

Billy looked at Jimmy and giggled; Jimmy looked at Billy and giggled; then, the latter took careful aim and a stream of water hit the old woman squarely in the face.

"Who dat? What's yo' doin'?" she yelled, as she backed off. "I's a-gwine to tell yo' pappy, Jimmy Garner," as she recognized one of the culprits. "P'int dat ar ho'e 'way f'om me, 'fo' I make yo' ma spank yuh slab-sided. I got to git home an' wash. Drap it, I tell yuh!"

Two little girls rolling two doll buggies in which reposed two enormous rag-babies were seen approaching.

"That's Lina Hamilton and Frances Black," said Jimmy; "they're my chums."

Billy took a good look at them. "They's goin' to be my chums, too," he said calmly.

"Your chums, nothing!" angrily cried Jimmy, swelling up pompously. "You all time trying to claim my chums. I can't have nothing a-tall 'thout you got to stick your mouth in. You 'bout the selfishest boy they is. You want everything I got, all time."

The little girls were now quite near and Jimmy hailed them gleefully, forgetful of his anger:

"Come on, Lina, you and Frances," he shrieked, "and we can have the mostest fun. Billy here's done come to live with Miss Minerva and she's done gone up town and don't care if we sprinkle, 'cause she's got so much 'ligion."

"But you know none of us are allowed to use a hose," objected Lina.

"But it's so much fun," said Jimmy; "and Miss Minerva she's so Christian she ain't going to raise much of a rough-house, and if she do we can run when we see her coming."

"I can't run," said Billy; "I ain't got no-where to run to an' —"

"If that ain't just like you, Billy," inter-

rupted Jimmy, "all time talking 'bout you
ain't got nowhere to run to; you don't want
nobody to have no fun. You 'bout the pica-
yunest boy they is."

Little Ikey Rosenstein, better known as
"Goose-Grease," dressed in a cast-off suit of
his big brother's, with his father's hat set
rakishly back on his head and over his ears,
was coming proudly down the street some
distance off.

"Yonder comes Goose-Grease Rosenstein," said Jimmy gleefully. "When he
gets right close le's make him hop."

"All right," agreed Billy, his good humor
restored, "le's baptize him good."

"Oh, we can't baptize him," exclaimed the
other little boy, "'cause he's a Jew and the
Bible says not to baptize Jews. You got to
mesmerize 'em. How come me to know
so much?" he continued condescendingly.
"Miss Cecilia teached me in the Sunday-

school.   Sometimes I know so much I feel
like I'm going to bust.   She teached me 'bout
'Scuffle little chillens and forbid 'em not,'
and 'bout 'Ananias telled Sapphira he done
it with his little hatchet,' and 'bout ''Lijah
jumped over the moon in a automobile.'   I
know everything what's in the Bible.   Miss
Cecilia sure is a cracker-jack; she's 'bout the
stylishest Sunday-school teacher they is.''

"'Twas the cow jumped over the moon,"
said Frances, "and it isn't in the Bible; it's
in Mother Goose."

"And Elijah went to Heaven in a chariot
of fire," corrected Lina.

"And I know all 'bout Gabr'el," continued
Jimmy unabashed.   "When folks called him
to blow his trumpet he was under the hay-
stack fast asleep."

Ikey was quite near by this time to command the attention of the four children.

"Le's mesmerize Goose-Grease," yelled

Jimmy, as he turned the stream of water full upon him.

Frances, Lina, and Billy clapped their hands and laughed for joy.

With a terrified and angry shriek their victim, dripping water at every step, ran howling by his tormentors. When he reached a safe distance he turned around, shook a fist at them, and screamed back:

"My papa is going to have you all arrested and locked up in the calaboose."

"Calaboose, nothing!" jeered Jimmy. "You all time wanting to put somebody in the calaboose 'cause they mesmerize you. You got to be mesmerized 'cause it's in the Bible."

A short, stout man, dressed in neat black clothes, was coming toward them.

"Oh, that's the Major!" screamed Billy delightedly, taking the hose and squaring himself to greet his friend of the train, but

Jimmy jerked it out of his hand, before either of them noticed him turning about, as if for something forgotten.

"You ain't got the sense of a one-eyed tadpole, Billy," he said. "That's Miss Minerva's beau. He's been loving her more'n a million years. My mama says he ain't never going to marry nobody a-tall 'thout he can get Miss Minerva, and Miss Minerva she just turns up her nose at anything that wears pants. You better not sprinkle him. He's been to the war and got his big toe shot off. He kilt 'bout a million Injuns and Yankees and he's name' Major 'cause he's a Confed'rit vetrun. He went to the war when he ain't but fourteen."

"Did he have on long pants?" asked Billy. "I call him Major Minerva—"

"Gladys Maude's got the pennyskeeters," broke in Frances importantly, fussing over her baby, "and I'm going to see Doctor

Sanford. Don't you think she looks pale, Jimmy?"

"Pale, nothing!" sneered the little boy. "Girls got to all time play their dolls are sick. Naw; I don't know nothing a-tall 'bout your Gladys Maude."

Lina gazed up the street.

"That looks like Miss Minerva to me 'way up yonder," she remarked. "I think we had better get away from here before she sees us."

Two little girls rolling two doll buggies fairly flew down the street and one little boy quickly climbed to the top of the dividing fence. From this safe vantage point he shouted to Billy, who was holding the nozzle of the hose.

"You'd better turn that water off 'cause Miss Minerva's going to be madder'n a green persimmon."

"I do' know how to," said Billy forlornly. "You turnt it on."

"Drop the hose and run to the hydrant and twist that little thing at the top," screamed Jimmy. "You all time got to perpose someping to get little boys in trouble anyway," he added ungenerously.

"You perposed this yo'self," declared an indignant Billy. "You said Aunt Minerva's so 'ligious she wouldn't git mad."

"Christian womans can get just as mad as any other kind," declared the other boy, sliding from his perch on the fence and running across his lawn to disappear behind his own front door.

Holding her skirts nearly up to her knees Miss Minerva stepped gingerly along the wet and muddy street till she got to her gate, where her nephew met her, looking a little guilty, but still holding his head up with that characteristic manly air which was so attractive.

"William," she said sternly, "I see you

have been getting into mischief, and I feel it my duty to punish you, so that you may learn to be trustworthy. I said nothing to you about the hose because I did not think you would know how to use it."

Billy remained silent. He did not want to betray his little companions of the morning, so he said nothing in his own defense.

"Come with me into the house," continued his aunt; "you must go to bed at once."

But the child protested vigorously.

"Don' make me go to bed in the daytime, Aunt Minerva; me an' Wilkes Booth Lincoln ain't never went to bed in the daytime sence we's born, an' I ain't never hear tell of a real 'ligious 'oman a-puttin' a little boy in bed 'fore it's dark; an' I ain't never a-goin' to meddle with yo' ole hose no mo'."

But Miss Minerva was obdurate, and the little boy spent a miserable hour between the sheets.

CHAPTER VI

SUCCESSFUL STRATEGY

"I HAVE a present for you," said his aunt, handing Billy a long, rectangular package.

"Thank you, ma'am," said her beaming nephew as he sat down on the floor, all eager anticipation, and began to untie the string. His charming, changeful face was bright and happy again, but his expression became one of indignant amaze as he saw the contents of the box.

"What I want with a doll?" he asked angrily; "I ain't no girl."

"I think every little boy should have a doll and learn to make clothes for it," said Miss Minerva. "I don't want you to be a great, rough boy; I want you to be sweet and gentle like a little girl; I am going to teach you how to sew and cook and sweep, so you may grow up a comfort to me."

This was a gloomy forecast for the little boy, accustomed, as he had been, to the freedom of a big plantation, and he scowled darkly.

"Me an' Wilkes Booth Lincoln ain't never hafter play with no dolls sence we's born," he replied sullenly; "we goes in swimmin' an' plays baseball. I can knock a home-run an' pitch a curve an' ketch a fly. Why don't you gimme a baseball bat? I already got a ball what Admiral Farragut gimme. An' I ain't a-goin' to be no sissy neither. Lina an' Frances plays dolls. Me an' Jimmy—" He stopped in sudden confusion.

"Lina and Frances and James!" exclaimed his aunt. "What do you know about them, William?"

The child's face flushed. "I seen 'em this mornin'," he acknowledged.

Miss Minerva put a hand on either shoulder and looked straight into his eyes.

"William, who started that sprinkling this morning?" she questioned, sharply.

Billy flushed guiltily and lowered his eyelids; but only for an instant. Quickly recovering his composure, he returned her gaze steadily and ignored her question.

"I see yo' beau, too, Aunt Minerva," he remarked tranquilly.

It was Miss Minerva this time who lost her composure, for her thin, sallow face became perfectly crimson.

"My beau?" she asked confusedly. "Who put that nonsense into your head?"

"Jimmy show him to me," he replied jauntily, once more master of the situation and in full realization of the fact. "Why don't you marry him, Aunt Minerva, so's he could live right here with us? An' I could learn him how to churn. I s'pec' he'd make

a beautiful churner. He sho' is a pretty little fat man," he continued flatteringly. "An'
dress? That beau was jest dressed plumb
up to the top notch. I sho' would marry
him if I's you an' not turn up my nose at
him 'cause he wears pants, an' you can learn
him how to talk properer'n what he do an'
I betcher he'd jest natchelly take to a broom,
an' I s'pec' he ain't got nobody't all to show
him how to sew. An' y' all could get the
doctor to fetch you a little baby so he
wouldn't hafter play with no doll. I sho'
wisht we had him here," ended a selfish
Billy; "he could save me a lot of steps. An'
I sho' would like to hear 'bout all them Injuns
an' Yankees what he's killed."

Billy's aunt was visibly embarrassed.

The persistent admiration of this, her one
lover, had been pleasing to her, yet she had
never been willing to sacrifice her independ-
ence for the cares and trials of matrimony.

The existing state of affairs between the two was known to every one in the small town, but such was Miss Minerva's dignified aloofness that Billy was the first person who had ever dared to broach the subject to her.

"Sit down here, William," she commanded, "and I will read to you."

"Tell me a tale," he said, looking up at her with his bright, sweet smile. The doll lay neglected on a chair near by and Billy wanted her to forget it.

"Tell me 'bout Piljerk Peter."

"Piljerk Peter?" There was an interrogation in her voice.

"Yas'm. Ain't you never hear tell 'bout Piljerk Peter? He had fifteen chillens an' one time the las' one of 'em an' his ole 'oman was down with the fever an' he ain't got but one pill an' they so sick they mos' 'bout to die an' ain't nobody in the fiel' fer to pick the cotton an' he can't git no doctor an' he ain't got but jest that one pill; so he tie that pill to a string an' let the bigges' chile swaller it an' draw it back up an' let the nex' chile swaller it an' jerk it back up an' let the nex' chile swaller it an' jerk it back up an' let the nex' chile swaller it an' jerk it back up an' let the nex' —"

"I don't believe in telling tales to children," interrupted his aunt; "I will tell you biographical and historical stories and stories from the Bible. Now listen, while I read to you."

"An' the nex' chile swaller it an' he jerk it back up," continued Billy serenely, "an' the nex' chile swaller it an' he jerk it back up tell finely ev'y single one of 'em, plumb down to the baby, swaller that pill an' the las' one of 'em got well an' that one pill it done the work. Then he tuck the pill and give it to his ole 'oman an' she swaller it an' he jerk it back up but didn't nothin' 't all come up but jest the string an' his ole 'oman she died 'cause all the strenk done gone outer that pill."

Miss Minerva opened a book called "Gems for the Household," which she had purchased from a silver-tongued book-agent. She selected an article the subject of which was "The Pure in Heart."

Billy listened with a seemingly attentive ear to the choice flow of words, but in reality his little brain was busy with his own thoughts. The article closed with the suggestion that if one were innocent and pure he would have a dreamless sleep:

> "If you have a conscience clear,
>   And God's commands you keep;
> If your heart is good and pure,
>   You will have a perfect sleep,"

Billy's aunt concluded. Wishing to know if he had understood what she had just read, she asked:

"What people sleep the soundest?"

"Niggers," was his prompt reply, as he thought of the long summer days and the colored folk on the plantation.

She was disappointed, but not discouraged.

"Now, William," she admonished, "I'm going to read you another piece, and I want you to tell me about it, when I get through. Pay strict attention."

"Yas'm," he readily agreed.

She chose an article describing the keen sense of smell in animals. Miss Minerva was not an entertaining reader and the words were long and fairly incomprehensible to the little boy sitting patiently at her side. Again his thoughts wandered, though every now and then he caught a word or two.

"What animals have the keenest sense of smell, William?" was her query at the conclusion of her reading.

"Billy goats," was Billy's answer without the slightest hesitation.

"You have goats on the brain," she said in anger. "I did not read one word about billy goats."

"Well, if 'tain't a billy goat," he replied, "I do' know what 'tis 'thout it's a skunk."

"I bought you a little primer this morning," she remarked after a short silence, "and I want you to say a lesson every day."

"I already knows a lot," he boasted. "Tabernicle, he an' Mercantile both been to school an' they learnt me an' Wilkes Booth Lincoln. I knows crooked S, an' broken back K, an' curly tail Q, an' roun' O, an' I can spell c-a-t cat, an' d-o-g dog an' A stands for apple."

That night he concluded his ever lengthy prayer at his kinswoman's knee with:

"O Lord, please make for Aunt Minerva a little baby—make her two of 'em. O Lord, if you got 'em to spare please make her three little babies an' let 'em all be girls so's she can learn 'em how to churn an' sew. An' bless Aunt Minerva and Major Minerva, f'r ever 'nd ever. Amen."

As he rose from his knees he asked: "Aunt Minerva, do God work on Sunday?"

"No-o," answered his relative, hesitatingly.

"Well, it look like He'd jest hafter work on Sunday, He's so busy jest a-makin' babies. He makes all the niggers an' heathens an' Injuns an' white chillens; I reckon He gits somebody to help him. Don't you, Aunt Minerva?"

CHAPTER VII

RABBITS' AND OTHER EGGS

ILLY was sitting in the swing. Jimmy crawled over the fence and joined him.

"Miss Cecilia's dyeing me some Easter eggs," he said, "all blue and pink and green and yelluh and every kind they is; I tooken her some of our hen's eggs and she is going to fix 'em for me and they'll be just like rabbit's eggs; I reckon I'll have 'bout a million. I'll give you one," he added generously.

"I want more 'n one," declared Billy, who was used to having the lion's share of everything.

"You all time talking 'bout you want more 'n one egg," said Jimmy. "You 'bout the stingiest Peter they is. Ain't you got no eggs? Get Miss Minerva to give you some of hers and I'll take 'em over and ask Miss Cecilia to dye 'em for you 'cause you ain't 'quainted with her yet."

"Aunt Minerva ain't got none 'cep'in' what she put under a ol' hen fer to set this mornin'."

"Can't you get 'em from under the old hen? Miss Minerva is such a Christian woman, she ain't—"

"You done fool me 'bout that 'ligious business befo'," interrupted Billy, "an' I got put to bed in the daytime."

"Well, she won't never miss two or three eggs," coaxed Jimmy. "How many did she put under the old hen?"

"She put fifteen," was the response, "an' I don't believe she'd want me to tech 'em."

"They're 'bout the prettiest eggs ever was," continued the tempter, "all blue and pink and green, and 'bout a million kinds.

They're just perzactly like rabbit's eggs.''

"Me an' Wilkes Booth Lincoln ain't never hear teller no rabbit's eggs sence we's born,'' said Billy; "I don't believe rabbits lays eggs nohow.''

"They don't lay 'em 'cept to Easter,'' said Jimmy. "Miss Cecilia 'splained it all to me and she's my Sunday-school teacher and rabbits is bound to lay eggs 'cause it's in the Bible and she's 'bout the prettiest 'splainer they is. I'm going over there now to see 'bout my eggs,'' and he made believe to leave the swing.

"Le's us slip roun' to the hen-house an' see what the ol' hen's a-doin','' suggested the sorely tempted Billy. "Aunt Minerva is a-makin' me some night-shirts an' she ain't takin' no notice of nothin' else.''

They tiptoed stealthily around the house to the back-yard, but found the hen-house door locked.

"Can't you get the key?" asked the younger child.

"Naw, I can't," replied the other boy; "but you can git in th'oo this-here little hole what the chickens goes in at, whiles I watches fer Aunt Minerva. I'll stand right here an' hol' my cap whiles you fetches me the eggs. An' don't you take more'n five or six," he warned.

"I'm skeered of the old hen," objected Jimmy. "Is she much of a pecker?"

"Naw, she ain't a-goin' to hurt you," was the encouraging reply. "Git up an' crawl th'oo; I'll help you."

Billy, having overcome his scruples, now entered into the undertaking with great zest.

Jimmy climbed the chicken ladder, kicked his chubby legs through the aperture, hung suspended on his fat little middle for an instant, and finally, with much panting and tugging, wriggled his plump, round body into the hen-house. He walked over where a lonesome looking hen was sitting patiently on a nest. He put out a cautious hand and the hen promptly gave it a vicious peck.

"Billy," he called angrily, "you got to come in here and hold this old chicken; she's 'bout the terriblest pecker they is."

Billy stuck his head in the little square hole. "Go at her from behind," he suggested; "put yo' hand under her easy like, an' don' let her know what you's up to."

Jimmy tried to follow these instructions, but received another peck for his pains. He promptly mutinied.

"If you want any eggs," he declared, scowling at the face framed in the aperture, "you can come get 'em yourself. I done monkeyed with this chicken all I'm going to."

So Billy climbed up and easily got his lean little body through the opening. He dex-

terously caught the hen by the nape of the
neck, as he had seen Aunt Cindy do, while
Jimmy reached for the eggs.

"If we ain't done lef' my cap outside on
the groun'," said Billy. "What we goin' to
put the eggs in?"

"Well, that's just like you, Billy; you all
time got to leave your cap on the ground.
I'll put 'em in my blouse till you get outside and then I'll hand 'em to you. How
many you going to take?"

"We might just as well git 'em all now,"
said Billy. "Aunt Cindy say they's some
kinder hens won't lay no chickens 't all if
folks put they hands in they nests an' this
here hen looks like to me she's one of them
kind, so the rester the eggs'll jest be waste,
anyhow, 'cause you done put yo' han's in her
nes', an' a dominicker ain't a-goin' to stan'
no projeckin' with her eggs. Hurry up."

Jimmy carefully distributed the eggs in-

side his blouse, and Billy once more crawled
through the hole and stood on the outside
waiting, cap in hand, to receive them.

But the patient hen had at last raised her
voice in angry protest and set up a furious
cackling, which so frightened the little boy
on the inside that he was panic-stricken. He
caught hold of a low roost pole, swung himself up and, wholly unmindful of his blouse
full of eggs, pushed his lower limbs through
the hole and stuck fast. A pair of chubby,
sturdy legs, down which were slowly trick-
ling little yellow rivulets, and half of a
plump, round body were all that would go
through.

"Pull!" yelled the owner of the short fat
legs. "I'm stuck and can't go no furder.
Pull me th'oo, Billy."

About this time the defrauded fowl flew
from her nest and attempted to get out by
her rightful exit. Finding it stopped up by

a wriggling, squirming body, she perched herself on the little boy's neck and flapped her enraged wings in his face.

'Pull!" yelled the child again; "help me th'oo, Billy, 'fore this fool chicken pecks all the meat off 'm my bones."

Billy grabbed the sticky limbs and gave a valiant tug, but the body did not move an inch. Alas, Jimmy with his cargo of broken eggs was fast imprisoned.

"Pull again!" yelled the scared and angry child; "you 'bout the idjetest idjet they is if you can't do no better'n that."

Billy jerked with all his strength, but with no visible result.

"Pull harder! You no-count gump!" screamed the prisoner, beating off the hen with his hands.

The boy on the outside, who was strong for his years, braced himself and gave a mighty wrench of the other child's stout ex-

tremities. Jimmy howled in pain and gave
his friend an energetic kick.

"Lemme go!" he shrieked; "you old im-
pe'dunt backbiter. I'm going to tell Miss
Minerva you pulled my legs out by the
roots."

A small portion of the prisoner's blouse
was visible. Billy caught hold of it and
gave a strong jerk. There was a sound of
ripping and tearing and the older boy fell
sprawling on his back with a goodly portion
of the younger child's raiment clutched in
his hands.

"Now see what you done," yelled the victim of his energy; "you ain't got the sense
of a buffalo gnat. Oh! Oh! This hole is
'bout to cut my stomach open."

"Hush, Jimmy!" warned the other child.
"Don't make so much noise. Else Aunt
Minerva 'll hear you."

"I want her to hear me," screamed Jimmy.

"You'd like me to stay stuck in a chicken hole all night. Oh! Oh! Oh!"

The noise did indeed bring Billy's aunt out on a tour of investigation. She had to knock a plank off the hen-house with an axe before Jimmy's release could be accomplished. He was lifted down, red, angry, sticky, and perspiring, and was indeed a sight to behold.

"Billy got to all time perpose something to get little boys in trouble," he growled, "and got to all time get 'em stuck in a hole in a chicken-house."

"My nephew's name is William," corrected she.

"You perposed this here yo'self!" cried an indignant Billy. "Me an' Wilkes Booth Lincoln don' know nothin' 't all 'bout no rabbit's eggs sence we's born."

"It doesn't matter who proposed it," said his aunt firmly. "You are going to be pun-

ished, William. I have just finished one of
your night-shirts. Come with me and put
it on and go to bed. Jimmy, you go home
and show yourself to your mother."

"Pick up yo' shirt-tail offer the groun'
what I tore off, Jimmy," advised Billy, "an'
take it home to yo' ma. Aunt Minerva," he
pleaded, following mournfully behind her,
"please don't put me to bed; the Major he
don' go to bed no daytimes; I won't never
get me no mo' eggs to make rabbits' eggs
outer."

CHAPTER VIII

TELLERS OF TALES

THE days flew rapidly by. Miss Minerva usually attempted to train Billy all the morning, and by the mid-day dinner hour she was so exhausted that she was glad to let him play in the front yard during the afternoon.

Here he was often joined by, the three children whose acquaintance he had made the day after his arrival, and the quartette became staunch friends and chums.

All four were sitting in the swing one warm spring day, under the surveillance of Billy's aunt, sewing on the veranda.

"Let's tell tales," suggested Jimmy.

"All right," agreed Frances. "I'll tell the first. Once there's—"

"Naw, you ain't neither," interrupted the

little boy. "You all time talking 'bout you going to tell the first tale. I'm going to tell the first tale myself. One time they's—"

"No you are not, either," said Lina positively. "Frances is a girl and she ought to be the first if she wants to. Don't you think so, Billy?"

"Yes, I does," championed he; "go on, Frances."

That little girl, thus encouraged, proceeded to tell the first tale.

"Once there's a man named Mr. Elisha, and he had a friend named Mr. Elijah, so his mantelpiece fell on top of his head and make him perfectly bald; he hasn't got a single hair and he hasn't got any money, 'cause mama read me 'bout he rented his garments, which is clo'es, 'cause he didn't have none at all what belong to him. I s'pec' he just rented him a shirt and a pair o' breeches and wore 'em next to his hide 'thout no under-

shirt at all. He was drea'ful poor and had a
miser'ble time and old mean Mr. Per'dven-
ture took him up on a high mountain and
left him, so when he come down some bad
little childern say, 'Go 'long back, bald
head!' and they make pock-mocks on him.
Seems like everybody treat him bad, so he
cuss 'em, so I never see anybody with a bald
head 'thout I run, 'cause I don't want to get
cussed. So two Teddy bears come out of
the woods and ate up forty-two hundred of
'em."

"Why, Frances," reproved Lina, "you always get things wrong. I don't believe they
ate up that many children."

"Yes they did, too," championed Jimmy,
"'cause it's in the Bible and Miss Cecilia
'splained all 'bout it to me, and she's our
Sunday school teacher and 'bout the bully-
est 'splainer they is. Them Teddy bears ate
up 'bout a million chillens, which is all the

little boys and girls two Teddy bears can hold at a time."

"I knows a man what ain't got no hair 't all on his head," remarked Billy; "he's a conjure-man an' me an' Wilkes Booth Lincoln been talkin' to him ever sence we's born an' he ain't never cuss us, an' I ain't never got eat up by no Teddy bears neither. Huccome him to be bald? He's out in the fiel' one day a-pickin' cotton when he see a tu'key buzzard an' he talk to her like this:

"'I say, tu'key buzzard, I say,

Who shall I see unexpected to-day?'

"If she flop her wings three times you goin' to see yo' sweetheart, but this-here buzzard ain't flop no wings 't all; she jes' lean over an' th'ow up on his head an' he been bald ever sence; ev'y hair come out."

"Did you-all hear 'bout that 'Talian Dago that works on the section gang eating a buzzard?" asked Frances.

"Naw," said Billy. "Did it make him sick?"

"That it did," she answered; "he sent for Doctor Sanford and tells him, 'Me killa de big bird; me eat-a de big bird; de big bird make-a me seek.'"

"Them Dagoes 'bout the funniest talking folks they is," said Jimmy, "but they got to talk that way 'cause it's in the Bible. They 'sputed on the tower of Babel and the Lord say 'Confound you!' Miss Cecilia 'splained it all to me and she's 'bout the dandiest 'splainer they is."

"You may tell your tale now, Jimmy," said Lina.

"I'm going to tell 'bout William Tell 'cause he's in the Bible," said Jimmy. "Once they's a man name'—"

"William Tell isn't in the Bible," declared Lina.

"Yes he is, too," contended the little boy;

"Miss Cecilia 'splained it to me. You all time setting yourself up to know more'n me and Miss Cecilia. One time they's a man name' William Tell and he had a little boy what's the cutest kid they is and the Devil come 'long and temp' him. Then the Lord say, 'William Tell, you and Adam and Eve can taste everything they is in the garden 'cepting this one apple tree; you can get all the pears and bunnanas and peaches and grapes and oranges and plums and persimmons and scalybarks and fig leaves and 'bout a million other kinds of fruit if you want to, but don't you tech a single apple.' And the Devil temp' him and say he going to put his cap on a pole and everybody got to bow down to it for a idol and if William Tell don't bow down to it he got to shoot a apple for good or evil off'm his little boy's head. That's all the little boy William Tell and Adam and Eve got, but he ain't going

to fall down and worship no gravy image
on top a pole, so he put a tomahawk in his
bosom and he tooken his bow and arruh and
shot the apple plumb th'oo the middle and
never swinge a hair of his head. And Eve
nibble off the apple and give Adam the core,
and Lina all time 'sputing 'bout Adam and
Eve and William Tell ain't in the Bible.
They're our first parents."

"Now, Billy, you tell a tale and then it
will be my time," said Lina with a saving-
the-best-for-the-last air.

"Once they was a ol' witch," said Billy,
"what got outer her skin ev'y night an' lef'
it on the he'rth an' turnt herself to a great,
big, black cat an' go up the chim'ly an' go
roun' an' ride folks fer horses, an' set on
ev'body's chis' an' suck they breath an'
kill 'em an' then come back to bed. An'
can't nobody ketch her tell one night her
husban' watch her an' he see her jump outer

her skin an' drop it on the he'rth an' turn to a 'normous black cat an' go up the chim'ly. An' he got outer the bed an' put some salt an' pepper an' vinegar on the skin an' she come back an' turnt to a 'oman an' try to git back in her skin an' she can't 'cause the salt an' pepper an' vinegar mos' burn her up, an' she keep on a-tryin' an' she can't never snuggle inter her skin 'cause it keep on a burnin' worser'n ever, an' there she is a 'oman 'ithout no skin on. So she try to turn back into a cat an' she can't 'cause it's pas' twelve er'clock, an' she jest swivvle an' swivvle tell finely she jest swivvle all up. An' that was the las' of the ole witch an' her husban' live happy ever after. Amen."

"Once upon a time," said Lina, "there was a beautiful maiden and she was in love, but her wicked old parent wants her to marry a rich old man threescore and ten years old, which is 'most all the old you can get unless you are going to die; and the lovely princess said, 'No, father, you may cut me in the twain but I will never marry any but my true love.' So the wicked parent shut up the lovely maiden in a high tower many miles from the ground, and made her live on turnips and she had nothing else to eat; so one day when she was crying a little fairy flew in at the window and asked, 'Why do you weep, fair one?' And she said, 'A wicked parent hath shut me up and I can't ever see my lover any more.' So the fairy touched her head with her wand and told her to hang her hair out of the window, and she did and it reached the ground, and her lover, holding a rope ladder in one hand and playing the guitar and singing with the other, climbed up by her hair and took her down on the ladder and his big black horse was standing near, all booted and spurred, and they rode away through the forest to his castle, and there they lived happy ever after."

"How he goin' to clam' up, Lina," asked Billy, "with a rope ladder in one hand and his guitar in the other?"

"I don't know," was the dignified answer. "That is the way it is told in my fairy-tale book."

CHAPTER IX

CHANGING THE ETHIOPIAN

ILLY and Jimmy were sitting in the swing.

"What makes your hair curl just like a girl's?" asked the latter. "It's 'bout the curliest hair they is."

"Yes, it do," was Billy's mournful response. "It done worry me 'mos' to death. Ever sence me an' Wilkes Booth Lincoln's born we done try ev'ything fer to get the curl out. They was a Yankee man came 'long las' fall a-sellin' some stuff in a bottle what he call 'No-To-Kink' what he say would take the kink outer any nigger's head. An' Aunt Cindy bought a bottle fer to take the kink outer her hair an' me an' Wilkes Booth Lincoln put some on us heads an' it jes' made mine curlier'n what it was al-

ready. I's 'shame to go roun' folks with
my cap off, a-lookin' like a frizzly chicken.
Miss Cecilia say she like it though, an'
we's engaged. We's goin' to git married
soon's I puts on long pants."

"How long you been here, Billy?"

"Well, I don't know perzactly, but I been
to Sunday school four times. I got engaged
to Miss Cecilia that very firs' Sunday, but
she didn' know it tell I went over to her
house the nex' day an' tol' her 'bout it. She
say she think my hair is so pretty."

"Pretty nothin'," sneered his rival. "She
jus' stuffin' you fuller'n a tick with hot air.
It just makes you look like a girl. There's a
young lady come to spend a week with my
mama not long ago and she put somepin' on
her head to make it right yeller. She left
the bottle to our house and I know where 't
is. Maybe if you'd put some o' that on your
head 't would take the curl out."

"'T ain't nothin' a-goin' to do it no good," gloomily replied Billy. "'T would jest make it yeller'n what 't is now. Won't I be a pretty sight when I puts on long pants with these here yaller curls stuck on topper my head? I'd 'nuther sight ruther be bal'-headed."

"Benny Dick's got 'bout the kinkiest head they is."

Benny Dick was the two-year-old baby of Mrs. Garner's cook, Sarah Jane.

"It sho' is," replied Billy. "Wouldn't he look funny if he had yaller hair, 'cause his face is so black?"

"I know where the bottle is," cried Jimmy, snatching eagerly at the suggestion. "Let's go get it and put some on Benny Dick's head and see if it'll turn it yeller."

"Aunt Minerva don' want me to go over to yo' house," objected Billy.

"You all time talking 'bout Miss Minerva

won't let you go nowheres; she sure is im-
perdunt to you. You 'bout the 'fraidest boy
they is. . . . Come on, Billy," pleaded
Jimmy.

The little boy hesitated.

"I don't want to git Aunt Minerva's dan-
der up any more 'n I jest natchelly boun'
to," he said, following Jimmy reluctantly to
the fence; "but I 'll jes' take a look at that
bottle an' see ef it looks anything 't all like
'No-To-Kink.'"

Giggling mightily, they jumped the dividing fence and slipped with stealthy tread
around the house to Sarah Jane's cabin in
the back-yard.

Benny Dick was sitting on the floor before the open door, the entrance of which
was securely barricaded to keep him inside.
Sarah Jane was in the kitchen cooking supper; they could hear her happy voice raised
in religious melody; Mrs. Garner had not yet

returned from a card party; the coast was clear, and the time propitious.

Jimmy tiptoed to the house and soon returned with a big bottle of a powerful "blondine" in one hand and a stick of candy in the other.

"Benny Dick," he said, "here's a nice stick of candy for you if you'll let us wash your head."

The negro baby's thick, red lips curved in a grin of delight, his shiny ebony face beamed happily, his round black eyes sparkled as he held out his fat, rusty little hands. He sucked greedily at the candy as the two mischievous little boys uncorked the bottle and poured a generous supply of the liquid on his head. They rubbed it in well, grinning with delight. They made a second and a third application before the bottle was exhausted; then they stood off to view the result of their efforts. The effect was ludicrous. The combination of coal black skin and red gold hair presented by the little negro exceeded the wildest expectations of Jimmy and Billy. They shrieked with laughter and rolled over and over on the floor in their unbounded delight.

"Hush!" warned Jimmy suddenly. "I believe Sarah Jane's coming out here to see 'bout Benny Dick. Let's get behind the door and see what she's going to do."

> "'Hit were good fer Paul an' Silas,
> Hit were good fer Paul an' Silas,
> Hit were good fer Paul an' Silas,
> An' hit's good ernough fer me,'"

floated Sarah Jane's song nearer and nearer.

> "'Hit's de ole time erligion,
> Hit's de old time—'"

She caught sight of her baby with his glistening black face and golden hair. She threw up her hands, closed her eyes, and uttered a terrified shriek. Presently she slowly opened her eyes and took a second peep at her curious-looking offspring. Sarah Jane screamed aloud.

"Hit's de handiwork er de great Jehoshaphat! Hit's de Marster's sign. Who turnt yo' hair, Benny Dick?" she asked of the sticky little pickaninny sitting happily on the floor. "Is a angel been here?"

Benny Dick nodded his head with a delighted grin of comprehension.

"Hit's de doing er de Lord," cried his mother. "He gwine turn my chile white an' he done begunt on his head!"

There was an ecstatic giggle from behind the door.

Sarah Jane rushed inside as fast as her mammoth proportions would admit and caught a squirming culprit in each huge black paw.

"What yer up ter now, Jimmy Garner?"
she asked. "What yer been er-doing?"

Sudden suspicion entered her mind as she
caught sight of the empty bottle lying on a
chair. "You been er-puttin' suthin' on my
chile's head! I knows yer. I's er-gwyne ter
make yo' mammy gi' ye de worses' whippin'
yer eber got an' I's gwine ter take dis here
William right over ter Miss Minerva. Ain't
y' all 'shame' er yerselves? Er tamperin'
wid de ha'r what de good Lord put on er
colored pusson's head an' er-tryin' fer ter
scarify my feelin's like yer done. An' yer
hear me, I's gwine see dat somebody got ter
scarify yer hides."

"If that ain't just like you, Billy," said
Jimmy: "you all time got to perpose to make
nigger heads yeller and you all time getting
little boys in trouble. You 'bout the smart
Alexest jack-rabbit they is."

"You perposed this here hair business

yo'self, Jimmy," retorted his fellow-con-
spirator. "Yo's always blamin' yo' meanness on somebody else ever seηce you's
born."

"Hit don't matter who perposed hit," said
Sarah Jane firmly; "meanness has been did,
an' y' all gotter be structified on de place
pervided by natur' fer ter lem my chile
erlone."

CHAPTER X

'LO! THE POOR INDIAN

BILLY had just decided to run down to the livery stable to pay Sam Lamb a visit when the gate opened, and Lina and Frances, their beloved dolls in their arms, came skipping in.

Jimmy, who had had a difference with Billy and was in the sulks on his own side of the fence, immediately crawled over and joined the others in the swing. He was lonesome and the prospect of companionship was too alluring for him to nurse his anger longer.

"Aunt Minerva's gone to the Aid Society," remarked the host. "Don't y'all wish it met ev'y day 'stid er jes' meetin' ev'y Monday?"

"Yes, I do," agreed Frances; "you can have so much fun when our mamas go to the Aid. My mama's gone too, so she left me with Brother and he's writing a love letter to Ruth Shelton, so I slipped off."

"Mother has gone to the Aid, too," said Lina.

"My mama too," chimed in Jimmy; "she goes to the Aid every Monday and to card parties nearly all the time. She told Sarah Jane to 'tend to me and Sarah Jane's asleep. I heard her snoring. Ain't we glad there ain't no grown folks to meddle? Can't we have fun?"

"What'll we play?" asked Frances, who had deliberately stepped in a mud puddle on the way, and splashed mud all over herself. "Let's make mud pies."

"Naw, we ain't a-going to make no mud pies," objected Jimmy. "We can make mud pies all time when grown folks 'r' looking."

"Le's's play sumpin' what we ain't never play' sence we's born," put in Billy.

"I hope grandmother won't miss me," said Lina; "she's reading a very interesting book."

"Let's play Injun!" yelled Jimmy; "we ain't never play' Injun."

This suggestion was received with howls of delight.

"My mama's got a box of red stuff that she puts on her face when she goes to the card parties. She never puts none on when she just goes to the Aid. I can run home and get the box to make us red like Injuns," said Frances.

"My mother has a box of paint, too."

"I ain't never see Aunt Minerva put no red stuff on her face," grieved Billy.

"Miss Minerva, she don't never let the Major come to see her, nor go to no card parties is the reason," explained the younger boy; "she just goes to the Aid where they ain't no men, and you don't hafter put no red on your face at the Aid. We'll let you have some of our paint, Billy. My mama's got 'bout a million diff'ent kinds."

"We got to have pipes," was Frances's next suggestion.

"My papa's got 'bout a million pipes," boasted Jimmy; "but he got 'em all to the office, I spec'."

"Father has a meerschaum."

"Aunt Minerva ain't got no pipe."

"Miss Minerva's 'bout the curiousest woman they is," said Jimmy; "she ain't got nothing a-tall; she ain't got no paint and she ain't got no pipe."

"Ladies don't use pipes, and we can do without them anyway," said Lina; "but we must have feathers; all Indians wear feathers."

"I'll get my mama's duster," said Jimmy.

"Me, too," chimed in Frances.

Here Billy with flying colors came to the fore and redeemed Miss Minerva's waning reputation.

"Aunt Minerva's got a great, big buncher tu'key feathers an' I can git 'em right now," and the little boy flew into the house and was back in a few seconds.

"We must have blankets, of course," said Lina, with the air of one whose word is law; "mother has a genuine Navajo."

"I got a little bow'narruh what Santa Claus bringed me," put in Jimmy.

"We can use hatchets for tomahawks," continued the little girl. "Come on, Frances; let us go home and get our things and come back here to dress up. Run, Jimmy, get your things! You, too, Billy!" she commanded.

The children ran breathlessly to their homes near by and collected the different ar-

ticles necessary to transform them into pre-
sentable Indians.

They soon returned, Jimmy dumping his
load over the fence and tumbling after; and
the happy quartette sat down on the grass
in Miss Minerva's yard.   First the paint
boxes were opened and generously shared
with Billy, as with their handkerchiefs they
spread thick layers of rouge over their charming, bright, mischievous little faces.

The feather decoration was next in the
order of events.

"How we goin' to make these feathers
stick?" asked Billy.

They were in a dilemma till the resource-
ful Jimmy came to the rescue.

"Wait a minute," he cried; "I'll be back
'fore you can say 'Jack Robinson.'"

He rolled over the fence and was back
in a few minutes, gleefully holding up a
bottle.

"This muc'lage'll make 'em stick," he panted, almost out of breath.

Lina assumed charge of the head-dresses. She took Billy first, rubbed the mucilage well into his sunny curls, and filled his head full of his aunt's turkey feathers, leaving them to stick out awkwardly in all directions and at all angles. Jimmy and Frances, after robbing their mothers' dusters, were similarly decorated, and last, Lina, herself, was tastefully arrayed by the combined efforts of the other three.

At last all was in readiness.

Billy, regardless of consequences, had pinned his aunt's newest gray blanket around him and was viewing, with satisfied admiration, its long length trailing on the grass behind him; Lina had her mother's treasured Navajo blanket draped around her graceful little figure; Frances, after pulling the covers off of several beds and finding nothing to suit her fanciful taste, had snatched a gorgeous silk afghan from the leather couch in the library. It was an expensive affair of intricate pattern, delicate stitches, and beautiful embroidery with a purple velvet border and a yellow satin lining. She had dragged one corner of it through the mud puddle and torn a big rent in another place.

Jimmy was glorious in a bright red blanket, strutting about, carrying his little bow and arrow.

"I'm going to be the Injun chief," he boasted.

"I'm going to be a Injun chief, too," parroted Frances.

"Chief, nothing!" he sneered; "you all time trying to be a Injun chief. You 'bout the pompousest little girl they is. You can't be a chief nohow; you got to be a squash; Injun ladies 'r' name' squashes; me an'

Billy's the chiefs. I'm name' old Setting
Bull, hisself."

"You can't be named 'Bull,' Jimmy," reproved Lina; "it isn't genteel to say 'bull'
before people."

"Yes I am, too," he contended. "Setting
Bull's the biggest chief they is and I'm going
to be name' him."

"Well, I am not going to play then," said

Lina primly; "my mother wants me to be genteel, and 'bull' is not genteel."

"I tell you what, Jimmy," proposed Frances; "you be name' 'Setting Cow.' 'Cow' is genteel 'cause folks milk 'em."

"Naw, I ain't going to be name' no cow, neither," retorted the little Indian; "you all time trying to 'suade somebody to be name' 'Setting Cow.'"

"He can't be name' a cow,"—Billy now entered into the discussion—"'cause he ain't no girl. Why don' you be name' 'Settin' Steer'? Is 'steer' genteel, Lina?" he anxiously inquired.

"Yes, he can be named 'Sitting Steer,'" she granted. Jimmy agreeing to the compromise, peace was once more restored.

"Frances and Lina have got to be the squashes—" he began.

"It isn't 'squashes,' it is 'squaws,'" corrected Lina.

"Yes 't is squashes, too," persisted Jimmy, "'cause it's in the Bible and Miss Cecilia 'splained it to me and she's 'bout the high-steppingest 'splainer they is. Me and Billy is the chiefs," he shouted, capering around, "and you and Frances is the squashes and got to have papooses strop' to your back."

"Bennie Dick can be a papoose," suggested Billy.

"I'm not going to be a Injun squash if I got to have a nigger papoose strapped to my back!" cried an indignant Frances. "You can strap him to your own back, Billy."

"But I ain't no squash," objected that little Indian.

"We can have our dolls for papooses," said Lina, going to the swing where the dolls had been left. Billy pulled a piece of string from his pocket and the babies were safely strapped to their mothers' backs. With stately tread, headed by Sitting Steer, the

children marched back and forth across the
lawn in Indian file.

So absorbed were they in playing Indian
that they forgot the flight of time until their
chief suddenly stopped, all his brave valor
gone as he pointed with trembling finger up
the street.

That part of the Ladies' Aid Society which
lived in West Covington was bearing down
upon them.

"Yonder's our mamas and Miss Minerva," he whispered. "Now look what a
mess Billy's done got us in; he all time got
to perpose someping to get chillens in trouble
and he all time got to let grown folks ketch
'em."

"Aren't you ashamed to tell such a story,
Jimmy Garner?" cried Frances. "Billy
didn't propose any such thing. Come on,
let's run," she suggested.

"'Tain't no use to run," advised Jimmy.

"They're too close and done already see us. We boun' to get what's coming to us anyway, so you might jus' as well make 'em think you ain't 'fraid of 'em. Grown folks gotto all time think little boys and girls 'r' skeered of 'em, anyhow."

"Aunt Minerva'll sho' put me to bed this time," said Billy. "Look like ev'y day I gotter go to bed."

"Mother will make me study the catechism all day to-morrow," said Lina dismally.

"Mama'll lock me up in the little closet under the stairway," said Frances.

"My mama'll gimme 'bout a million licks and try to take all the hide off o' me," said Jimmy; "but we done had a heap of fun."

It was some hours later. Billy's aunt had ruthlessly clipped the turkey feathers from his head, taking the hair off in great patches. She had then boiled his scalp, so the little boy thought, in her efforts to remove the mucilage. Now, shorn of his locks and of some of his courage, the child was sitting quietly by her side, listening to a superior moral lecture and indulging in a compulsory heart-to-heart talk with his relative.

"I don't see that it does you any good, William, to put you to bed."

"I don' see as it do neither," quickly agreed Billy.

"I can not whip you; I am constitutionally opposed to corporal punishment for children."

"I's 'posed to it too," he assented.

"I believe I will hire a servant, so that I may devote my entire time to your training."

This prospect for the future did not appeal to her nephew. On the contrary, it filled him with alarm.

"A husban' d be another sight handier," he declared with energy; "he'd be a heap

mo' 'count ▓▓▓▓▓ a cook, Aunt Minerva.
There's that ▓▓▓▓▓—"

"You will never make a preacher of yourself, William, unless you improve."

The child looked up at her in astonishment; this was the first he knew of his being
destined for the ministry.

"A preacher what 'zorts an' calls up
mourners?" he said. "Not on yo' tin-type.
Me an' Wilkes Booth Lincoln—"

"How many times have I expressed the
wish not to have you bring that negro's
name into the conversation?" she impatiently interrupted.

"I don' perzactly know, 'm," he answered
good-humoredly. "'Bout fifty hunerd, I
reckon. Anyways, Aunt Minerva, I ain't
goin' to be no preacher. When I puts on
long pants I's goin' to be a Confedrit Vet-
'run an' kill 'bout fifty hunerd Yankees an'
Injuns, like my Major man."

HE children were sitting in the swing. Florence Hammer, a little girl whose mother was spending the day at Miss Minerva's, was with them.

"Don't you-all wish Santa Claus had his birthday right now 'stead o' waiting till Christmas to hang up our stocking?" asked Frances.

"Christmas isn't Santa Claus' birthday," corrected Lina. "God was born on Christmas and that's the reason we hang up our stockings."

"Yes; it is old Santa's birthday, too," argued Jimmy, "'cause it's in the Bible and Miss Cecelia 'splained it to me and she's 'bout the dandiest 'splainer they is."

"Which you all like the best: God or Doctor Sanford or Santa Claus?" asked Florence.

"I like God 'nother sight better'n I do anybody," declared Jimmy, "'cause He so forgivingsome. He's 'bout the forgivingest person they is. Santa Claus can't let you go to Heaven nor Doctor Sanford neither, nor our papas and mamas nor Miss Minerva. Now wouldn't we be in a pretty fix if we had to 'pend on Doctor Sanford or Santa Claus to forgive you every time you run off or fall down and bust your breeches. Naw; gimme God ev'y time."

"I like Santa Claus the best," declared Frances, "'cause he isn't f'rever getting in your way, and hasn't any castor oil like Doctor Sanford, and you don't f'rever have to be telling him you're sorry you did what you did, and he hasn't all time got one eye on you either, like God, and got to follow you 'round. And Santa Claus don't all time say, 'Shet your eyes and open your mouth,' like Doctor Sanford, 'and poke out your tongue.'"

"I like Doctor Sanford the best," said Florence, "'cause he's my uncle, and God and Santa Claus ain't kin to me."

"And the Bible say, 'Love your kinfolks.' Miss Cecilia 'splained—"

"I use to like my Uncle Doc' heap better'n what I do now," went on the little girl, heedless of Jimmy's interruption, "till I went with daddy to his office one day. And what you reckon that man's got in his office? He's got a dead man 'thout no meat nor clo'es on in there, nothing a-tall but just his bones."

"Was he a ha'nt?" asked Billy. "I like the Major best—he's got meat on."

"Naw; he didn't have no sheet on—just bones," was the reply.

"No sheet on; no meat on!" chirruped Billy, glad of the rhyme.

"Was he a angel, Florence?" questioned Frances.

"Naw; he didn't have no harp and no wings neither."

"It must have been a skeleton," explained Lina.

"And Uncle Doc' just keeps that poor man there and won't let him go to Heaven where dead folks b'longs."

"I spec' he wasn't a good man 'fore he died and got to go to the Bad Place," suggested Frances.

"I'll betcher he never asked God to forgive him when he 'ceived his papa and sassed his mama," — this from Jimmy, — "and Doctor Sanford's just a-keeping old Satan from getting him to toast on a pitchfork."

"I hope they'll have a Christmas tree at

Sunday school next Christmas," said Frances, harking back, "and I hope I'll get a heap o' things like I did last Christmas. Poor little Tommy Knott, he's so skeered he wasn't going to get nothing at all on the tree so he got him a great, big, red apple an' he wrote on a piece o' paper 'From Tommy Knott to Tommy Knott,' and tied it to the apple and put it on the tree for hisself."

"Let's ask riddles," suggested Lina.

"All right," shouted Frances, "I'm going to ask the first."

"Naw; you ain't neither," objected Jimmy. "You all time got to ask the first riddle. I'm going to ask the first one —
" 'Round as a biscuit, busy as a bee,
    Prettiest little thing you ever did see.' —
                    " 'A watch.'
" 'Humpty Dumpty sat on a wall,
    Humpty Dumpty had a great fall,

All the king's horses and all the king's
    men
Can't put Humpty Dumpty back again.'
                                    "'A egg.'
"'Round as a ring, deep as a cup,
    All the king's horses can't pull it up.'
                                    "'A well.'
"'House full, yard full, can't ketch—'"

"Hush, Jimmy!" cried Lina, in disgust.
"You don't know how to ask riddles. You
mustn't give the answers, too. Ask one
riddle at a time and let some one else
answer it. I'll ask one and see who can
answer it:

"'As I was going through a field of wheat
    I picked up something good to eat,
    'T was neither fish nor flesh nor bone,
    I kept it till it ran alone?'"

"A snake! A snake!" guessed Florence.
"That's a easy riddle."

"Snake, nothing!" scoffed Jimmy; "you can't eat a snake. 'Sides Lina wouldn't 'a' picked up a snake. Is it a little baby rabbit, Lina?"

"It was neither fish nor flesh nor bone," she declared; "and a rabbit is flesh and bone."

"Then it's boun' to be a apple," was Jimmy's next guess; "that ain't no flesh and blood and it's good to eat."

"An apple can't run alone," she triumphantly answered. "Give it up? Well, it was an egg and it hatched to a chicken. Now, Florence, you ask one."

"S'pose a man was locked up in a house," she asked, "how'd he get out?"

"Clam' outer a winder," guessed Billy.

"'Twa'n't no winder to the house," she declared.

"Crawled out th'oo the chim'ly, like Santa Claus," was Billy's next guess.

"'T wa'n't no chim'ly to it. Give it up?
Give it up?" the little girl laughed gleefully. "Well, he just broke out with
measles."

"It is Billy's time," said Lina, who seemed
to be mistress of ceremonies.

"Tabernicle learnt this here one at school;
see, if y' all can guess it. 'Tabby had four
kittens but Stillshee didn't have none 't
all.'"

"I don't see no sense a-tall in that,"
argued Jimmy, "'thout some bad little boys
drowned 'em."

"Tabby was a cat," explained the other
boy, "and she had four kittens; and Stillshee
was a little girl, and she didn't have no
kittens 't all."

"What's this?" asked Jimmy: "'A man
rode 'cross a bridge and Fido walked.' Had
a little dog name' Fido."

"You didn't ask that right, Jimmy," said

Lina; "you always get things wrong. The riddle is, 'A man rode across a bridge and Yet he walked,' and the answer is, 'He had a little dog named Yet who walked across the bridge.'"

"Well, I'd 'nother sight ruther have a little dog name' Fido," declared Jimmy. "A little dog name' Yet and a little girl name' Stillshee ain't got no sense a-tall to it."

"Why should a hangman wear suspenders?" asked Lina. "I'll bet nobody can answer that."

"To keep his breeches from falling off," triumphantly answered Frances.

"No, you goose, a hangman should wear suspenders so that he'd always have a gallows handy."

CHAPTER XII

IN THE HOUSE OF THE LORD

T was a beautiful Sunday morning.

The pulpit of the Methodist Church was not occupied by its regular pastor, Brother Johnson. Instead, a traveling minister, collecting funds for a church orphanage in Memphis, was the speaker for the day. Miss Minerva rarely missed a service in her own church. She was always on hand at the Love Feast and the Missionary Rally and gave liberally of her means to every cause. She was sitting in her own pew between Billy and Jimmy, Mr. and Mrs. Garner having remained at home. Across the aisle from her sat Frances Black, between her father and mother; two pews in front of her were Mr. and Mrs.

Hamilton, with Lina on the outside next the aisle. The good Major was there, too; it was the only place he could depend upon for seeing Miss Minerva.

The preacher, after an earnest and eloquent discourse from the text, "He will remember the fatherless," closed the big Bible with a bang calculated to wake any who might be sleeping. He came down from the pulpit and stood close to his hearers as he made his last pathetic appeal.

"My own heart," said he, "goes out to every orphan child, for in the yellow fever epidemic of '78, when but two years old, I lost both father and mother. If there are any little orphan children here to-day, I should be glad if they would come up to the front and shake hands with me."

Now Miss Minerva always faithfully responded to every proposal made by a preacher; it was a part of her religious conviction. At revivals she was ever a shining, if solemn and austere, light. When a minister called for all those who wanted to go to Heaven to rise, she was always the first on her feet. If he asked to see the raised hands of those who were members of the church at the tender age of ten years, Miss Minerva's thin, long arm gave a prompt response. Once when a celebrated evangelist was holding a big protracted meeting under canvas in the town and had asked all those who had read the book of Hezekiah in the Bible to stand up, Miss Minerva on one side of the big tent and her devoted lover on the other side were among the few who had risen to their feet. She had read the good book from cover to cover, from Genesis to Revelation over and over, so she thought she had read Hezekiah a score of times.

So now, when the preacher called for

little orphans to come forward, she leaned down and whispered to her nephew, "Go up to the front, William, and shake hands with the nice kind preacher."

"Wha' fer?" he asked. "I don' want to go up there; ev'ybody here'll look right at me."

"Are there no little orphans here?" the minister was saying. "I want to shake the hand of any little child who has had the misfortune to lose its parents."

"Go on, William," commanded his aunt. "Go shake hands with the preacher."

The little boy again demurred but, Miss Minerva insisting, he obediently slipped by her and by his chum. Walking gracefully and jauntily up the aisle to the spot where the lecturer was standing by a broad table, he held out his slim, little hand.

Jimmy looked at these proceedings of Billy's in astonishment, not comprehending at all. He was rather indignant that the older boy had not confided in him and invited his participation.

But Jimmy was not the one to sit calmly by and be ignored when there was anything doing, so he slid awkwardly from the bench before Miss Minerva knew what he was up to. Signaling Frances to follow, he swaggered pompously behind Billy and he, too, held out a short, fat hand to the minister.

The speaker smiled benignly down upon them; lifting them up in his arms, he stood the little boys upon the table. He thought the touching sight of these innocent and tender little orphans would empty the pockets of the audience. Billy turned red with embarrassment at his conspicuous position, while Jimmy grinned happily at the amused congregation. Horrified Miss Minerva half rose to her feet, but decided to remain where she was. She was a timid woman and did not know what course she ought to pursue. Besides, she had just caught the Major's smile.

"And how long have you been an orphan?" the interested preacher was asking of Billy.

"Ever sense me an' Wilkes Booth Lincoln 's born," sweetly responded the child.

"I 'bout the orphanest boy they is," volunteered Jimmy.

Frances, responding to the latter's invitation, had crawled over her father's legs before he realized what was happening. She, too, went sailing down the aisle, her stiff white dress standing straight up in the back like a strutting gobbler's tail. She grabbed hold of the man's hand, and was promptly lifted to the table beside the other "orphans." Tears stood in the good preacher's eyes as he turned to the tittering audience and said in a pathetic voice,

"Think of it, my friends, this beautiful little girl has no mother."

Poor Mrs. Black! A hundred pairs of eyes sought her pew and focused themselves upon the pretty young woman sitting there, red, angry, and shamefaced. Mr. Black was visibly amused and could hardly keep from laughing aloud.

As Frances passed by the Hamiltons' pew in her promenade down the aisle, Mrs. Hamilton leaned across her husband and made an attempt to clutch Lina, but she was too late; already that dignified little "orphan" was gliding with stately, conscious tread to join the others. This was too much for the audience. A few boys laughed out and for the first time the preacher's suspicions were aroused. As he clasped Lina's slender, graceful little hand he asked:

"And you have no father or mother, little girl?"

"Yes I have, too," she angrily retorted. "My father and mother are sitting right there," and she pointed a slim forefinger at her crimson, embarrassed parents.

CHAPTER XIII

JOB AND POLLIE BUMPUS

NEVER have told a downright falsehood," said Lina. "Mother taught me how wicked it is to tell stories. Did you ever tell a fib to your mother, Frances?"

"'Tain't no use to try to 'ceive my mama," was the reply of the other little girl; "she's got such gimlet eyes and ears she can tell with 'em shut if you're fibbing. I gave up hope long ago, so I just go 'long and tell her the plain gospel truth when she asks me, 'cause I know those gimlet eyes and ears of hers 're going to worm it out o' me somehow."

"Grown folks pin you down so close sometimes," said Jimmy, "you bound to 'varicate a little; and I always tell God I'm sorry. I

tell my mama the truth 'most all time 'cepting when she asks questions 'bout things
ain't none of her business a-tall, and she all
time want to know 'Who done it?' and if
. I let on it's me, I know she'll wear out
all the slippers and hair-brushes they is
paddling my canoe, 'sides switches, so I jus'
say 'I do' know, 'm'—which all time ain't
perzactly the truth. You ever tell Miss
Minerva stories, Billy?"

"Aunt Cindy always say, 'twa'n't no
harm 'tall to beat 'bout the bush an' try to
th'ow folks offer the track 'long as you can,
but if it come to the point where you got to
tell a out-an'-out fib, she say for me always
to tell the truth, an' I jest natchelly do like
she tell me to ever sence I's born," replied
Billy.

The children swung awhile in silence.
Presently Jimmy broke the quiet by remarking:

"Don't you all feel sorry for old Miss Pollie Bumpus? She live all by herself, and she 'bout a million years old, and Doctor Sanford ain't never brung her no chillens 'cause she ain't got 'er no husban' to be their papa, and she got a octopus in her head, and she poor as a post and deaf as Job's old turkey-hen."

"Job's old turkey-hen wasn't deaf," retorted Lina primly; "she was very, very poor and thin."

"She was deaf, too," insisted Jimmy, "'cause it's in the Bible. I know all 'bout Job," bragged he.

"I know all 'bout Job, too," chirped Frances.

"Job, nothing!" said Jimmy, with a sneer; "you all time talking 'bout you know all 'bout Job; you 'bout the womanishest little girl they is. Now I know Job 'cause Miss Cecilia 'splained all 'bout him to me. He's

in the Bible and he sold his birthmark for
a mess of potatoes and—"

"You never can get anything right,
Jimmy," interrupted Lina; "that was Esau
and it was not his birthmark; it was his
birthstone; and he sold his birthstone for a
mess of potash."

"Yes," agreed Frances; "he saw Esau
kissing Kate and Esau had to sell him his
birthstone to keep his mouth shut."

"Mother read me all about Job," continued Lina; "he was afflicted with boils and
his wife knit him a Job's comforter to wrap
around him, and he—"

"And he sat under a 'tato vine," put in
Frances eagerly, "what God grew to keep
the sun off o' his boils and —"

"That was Jonah," said Lina, "and it
wasn't a potato vine; it was—"

"No, 'twasn't Jonah neither; Jonah is
inside of a whale's bel—"

"Frances!"

"Stommick," Frances corrected herself, "and a whale swallow him, and how's he going to sit under a pumpkin vine when he's inside of a whale?"

"It was not a pumpkin vine, it—"

"And I'd jus' like to see a man inside of a whale a-setting under a morning-glory vine."

"The whale vomicked him up," said Jimmy.

"What sorter thing is a octopus like what y'all say is in Miss Pollie Bumpus's head?" asked Billy.

"'Tain't a octopus; it's a polypus," explained Frances, "'cause she's named Miss Pollie. It's a something that grows in your nose and has to be named what you's named. She's named Miss Pollie and she's got a polypus."

"I'm mighty glad my mama ain't got no

Eva-pus in her head," was Jimmy's comment. "Ain't you glad, Billy, your Aunt Minerva ain't got no Miss Minerva-pus?"

"I sho' is," fervently replied Miss

Minerva's nephew; "she's hard 'nough to manage now like she is."

"I'm awful good to Miss Pollie," said Frances. "I take her someping good to eat 'most every day. I took her two pieces of pie this morning; I ate up one piece on the way and she gimme the other piece when I got there. I jus' don't believe she could get 'long at all 'thout me to carry her the good things to eat that my mama sends her; I takes her pies all the time; she says they're the best smelling pies ever she smelt."

"You 'bout the piggiest girl they is," said Jimmy; "all time got to eat up a poor old woman's pies. You'll have a Frances-pus in your stomach first thing you know."

"She's got a horn that you talk th'oo," continued the little girl, serenely contemptuous of Jimmy's adverse criticism, "and 'fore I knew how you talk into it, she says to me one day, 'How's your ma?' and stuck that old horn at me; so I put it to my ear, too, and there we set; she got one end of the horn to her ear and I got the other end to my ear; so when I saw this wasn't going to work I took it and blew into it; you-all'd died a-laughing to see the way I did. But now I can talk th'oo it's good's anybody."

"That is an ear trumpet, Frances," said Lina; "it is not a horn."

"Le's play 'Hide the Switch,'" suggested Billy.

"I'm going to hide it first," cried Frances.

"Naw, you ain't," objected Jimmy; "you all time got to hide the switch first. I'm going to hide it first myself."

"No, I'm going to say 'William Com Trimbleton,'" said Frances, "and see who's going to hide it first. Now you-all spraddle out your fingers."

CHAPTER XIV

MR. ALGERNON JONES

GAIN was it Monday, with the Ladies' Aid Society in session. Jimmy was sitting on the grass in his own front yard, in full view of Sarah Jane, who was ironing clothes in her cabin, with strict orders to keep him at home. Billy was in the swing in Miss Minerva's yard.

"Come on over," he invited.

"I can't," was the reply across the fence; "I'm so good now I 'bout got 'ligion; I reckon I'm going to be a mish-nary or a pol'tician, one or t'other when I'm a grown-up man 'cause I'm so good; I ain't got but five whippings this week. I been good ever since I let you 'suade me to play Injun. I'm the goodest little boy in this town, I 'spec'. Sometimes I get scared 'bout being so good 'cause I hear a woman say if you too good, you going to die or you ain't got no sense, one. You come on over here; you ain't trying to be good like what I'm trying, and Miss Minerva don't never do nothing a-tall to you 'cepting put you to bed."

"I'd ruther to git whipped fifty hunderd times 'n to hafter go to bed in the daytime with Aunt Minerva lookin' at you. An' her specs can see right th'oo you plumb to the bone. Naw, I can't come over there 'cause she made me promise not to. I ain't never go back on my word yit."

"I hope mama won't never ask me to promise her nothing a-tall, 'cause I'm mighty curious 'bout forgetting. I 'spec' I'm the most forgettingest little boy they is. But I'm so glad I'm so good. I ain't never going to be bad no more; so you might just as well quit begging me to come over and swing. You needn't ask me no more,—'t ain't no use a-tall."

"I ain't a-begging you," cried Billy contemptuously; "you can set on yo' mammy's grass where you is, an' be good from now tell Jedgment Day an' 'twon't make no change in my business."

"I ain't going to be 'ticed into no meanness, 'cause I'm so good," continued the reformed one, after a short silence during which he had seen Sarah Jane turn her back to him, "but I don't b'lieve it'll be no harm jus' to come over and set in the swing with you; maybe I can 'fluence you to be good like me and keep you from 'ticing little boys into mischief. I think I'll just come over and set a while and help you to be good," and he started to the fence. Sarah Jane turned around in time to frustrate his plans.

"You git right back, Jimmy," she yelled;

"you git erway f'om dat-ar fence an' quit confabbin' wid dat-ar Willyum. Fixin' to make some mo' Injuns out o' yo'selfs, ain't yeh, or some yuther kin' o' skeercrows?"

Billy strolled to the other side of the big yard and climbed up and sat on the tall gate post. A stranger, coming from the opposite direction, stopped and spoke to him.

"Does Mr. John Smith live here?" he asked.

"Naw, sir," was the reply; "don't no Mr. 'tall live here; jest me an' Aunt Minerva, an' she turns up her nose at anything that wears pants."

"And where could I find your Aunt Minerva?" The stranger's grin was ingratiating and agreeable.

"Why, this here's Monday," the little boy exclaimed. "Of course she's at the Aid; all the 'omans roun' here goes to the Aid on Monday."

"Your aunt is an old friend of mine," went on the man, "and I knew she was at the Aid. I just wanted to find out if you'd tell the truth about her. Some little boys tell stories, but I am glad to find out you are so truthful. My name is Mr. Algernon Jones and I'm glad to know you. Shake! Put it there, partner," and the fascinating stranger held out a grimy paw.

Billy smiled down from his perch at him and thought he had never met such a pleasant man. If he was such an old friend of his aunt's maybe she would not object to him because he wore pants, he thought. Maybe she might be persuaded to take Mr. Jones for a husband. Billy almost hoped that she would hurry home from the Aid, he wanted to see the two together so.

"Is you much of a cusser?" he asked solemnly, "'cause if you is you'll hafter cut it out on these premises."

Mr. Jones seemed much surprised and hurt at the question.

"An oath never passed these lips," replied the truthful gentleman.

"Can you churn?"

"Churn—churn?" with a reminiscent smile; "I can churn like a top."

Jimmy was dying of curiosity but the gate was too far away for him to do more than catch a word now and then. It was also out of Sarah Jane's visual line, so she knew nothing of the stranger's advent.

"And you're here all by yourself?" insinuated Billy's new friend. "And the folks next door, where are they?"

"Mrs. Garner's at the Aid an' Mr. Garner's gone to Memphis. That is they little boy a-settin' in they yard on they grass," answered the child.

"I've come to fix your Aunt Minerva's water pipe," said truth-loving Mr. Jones.

"Come, show me the way; I'm the plumber."

"In the bathroom?" asked the child. "I didn't know it needed no fixin'."

He led the agreeable plumber through the hall, down the long back-porch to the bathroom, remarking:

"I'll jes' watch you work." And he seated himself in the only chair.

Here is where Billy received one of the greatest surprises of his life. The fascinating stranger grabbed him with a rough hand and hissed:

"Don't you dare open your mouth or I'll crack your head open, and scatter your brains. I'll eat you alive."

The fierce, bloodshot eyes, which had seemed so laughing and merry before, now glared into those of the little boy as the man took a stout cord from his pocket, bound Billy to the chair, and gagged him with a large bath towel. Energetic Mr.

Jones took the key out of the door, shook his fist at the child, went out, and locked the door behind him.

Jimmy, seeing no hope of eluding Sarah Jane's vigilance, resorted to strategy and deceit.

"'Tain't no fun setting out here," he called to her, "so I'm going in the house and take a nap."

She willingly consented, as she was through with her ironing, and thought to snatch a few winks of sleep herself.

The little boy slipped quietly through the house, noiselessly across the back-yard and into his father's big garden, which was separated from that of his neighbor by a high board-fence. He quickly climbed the fence, flew across Miss Minerva's tomato patch and tiptoed up her back steps to the back-porch, his little bare feet giving no sign of his presence. Hearing curious noises com-

ing from the bathroom, where Billy was
bumping the chair up and down in his efforts
to release his mouth, he made for that spot,
promptly unlocked the door, and walked in.
Billy by scuffling and tugging had at that
moment freed his mouth from the towel.

"Hush!" he whispered as Jimmy opened
the door; "you'll get eat up alive if you
don't look out." His tone was so myste-
rious and thrilling and he looked so scared
tied to the chair that the younger boy's
blood almost froze in his veins.

"What you doing all tied up so?" he asked
in low, frightened tones.

"Mr. Algernon Jones done it. I spec' he's
a robber an' jes' a-robberin' right now."

"I'll untie you," said his chum.

"Naw; you better not," said Billy bravely.
"He might git away. You leave me jes' like
he fixed me so's you can try to ketch him.
I hear him in the dinin'-room now. You

leave me right here an' step over to yo' house an' 'phone to some mens to come and git him quick. Shet the do' ag'in an' don't make no noise. Fly, now!"

And Jimmy did fly. He again took the garden route and in a minute was at the telephone with the receiver at his ear.

"Hello! Is that you, Miss Central? This is me," he howled into the transmitter. "Gimme Miss Minerva's beau. I don't know his number, but he's got a office over my papa's bank."

His father being out of town, the little boy shrewdly decided that Miss Minerva's beau was the next best man to help.

"Miss Minerva what lives by me," he shrieked.

Fortunately Central recognized his childish voice and was willing to humor him, so as she too knew Miss Minerva's beau the connection was quickly made.

"Hello! Is that you, Major? This is me. If you don't want Mr. Algernon Jones to be robbering everything Miss Minerva's got you better get a move on and come right this minute. You got to hustle and bring 'bout a million pistols and guns and swords and tomahawks and all the mans you can find and dogs. He's the fiercest robber ever was, and he's already done tie Billy to a bathroom chair and done eat up 'bout a million cold biscuits, I spec'. All of us is 'bout to be slewed. Good-bye."

The plump, round gentleman at the other end of the wire heard this amazing message in the utmost confusion and consternation. He frantically rang the telephone again and again but could get no answer from the Garners' home so he put on his hat and walked the short distance to Miss Minerva's house.

Jimmy was waiting to receive him at the

front gate, having again eluded Sarah Jane's vigilance.

"Hush!" he whispered mysteriously, "he's in the dining-room. Ain't you bringed nobody else? Get your pistol and come on."

Mr. Algernon Jones, feeling safe and secure for the next hour and having partaken of a light lunch, was in the act of transferring some silver spoons from the sideboards to his pockets when a noise at the dining-room door caused him to look in that direction. With an oath he sprang forward, and landed his fist upon the nose of a plump gentleman standing there, bringing a stream of blood and sending him sprawling to the floor. Mr. Jones overturned a big-eyed little boy who was in his way and, walking rapidly in the direction of the railroad, the erstwhile plumber was seen no more.

Jimmy quickly recovered himself and sprang to his feet. Seeing the blood streaming down the white shirt front of Miss Minerva's unconscious beau, he gathered his wits together and took the thread of events again into his own little hands. He flung himself over the fence, careless of Sarah Jane this time, mounted a chair and once more rang the telephone.

"Hello! Is that you, Miss Central? This is me some more. Gimme Doctor Sanford's office, please.

"Hello! Is that you, Doctor? This is me. Mr. Algernon Jones done kilt Miss Minerva's beau. He's on her back-porch bloody all over. He's 'bout the deadest man they is. You'd better come toreckly you can and bring the hearse, and a coffin and a clean shirt and a tombstone. He's wounded me but I ain't dead yet. Goodbye."

Doctor Sanford received Jimmy's crazy message in astonishment. He, too, rang the telephone again and again but could hear nothing more, so he walked down to Miss Minerva's house and rang the door-bell. Jimmy opened the door and led the way to the back-porch, where the injured man, who had just recovered consciousness, was sitting limply in a chair.

"What does all this mean? Are you hurt?" asked the Doctor as he examined Mr. Jones's victim.

"No, I think I'm all right now," was the reply; "but that scoundrel certainly gave me a severe blow."

Billy, shut up in the bathroom and listening to all the noise and confusion, had been scared nearly out of his senses. He had kept as still as a mouse till now, when, thinking he heard friendly voices, he yelled out, "Open the do' an' untie me."

"We done forgot Billy," said the little rescuer, as he ran to the bathroom door and opened it. He was followed by the Doctor, who cut the cords that bound the prisoner.

"Now, William," commanded Doctor Sanford as they grouped themselves around the stout, plump gentleman in the chair, "begin at the beginning, and let us get at the bottom of this affair."

"Mr. Algernon Jones he come to the gate," explained the little boy, "an' he say he goin' to fix the water pipe an' he say he's a plumber. He's a very 'greeable man, but I don't want Aunt Minerva to marry him, now. I was plumb tickled at him an' I tuck him to the bathroom an' fust thing I knowed he grabbed holter me an' shuck me like what you see a cat do a mouse, an' he say—"

"And he'd more'n a million whiskers," interrupted Jimmy, who thought Billy was receiving too much attention, "and he—"

"One at a time," said the Doctor. "Proceed, William."

"An' he say he'll bust my brains outer my head if I holler, an' I ain't a-goin' to holler neither, an' he tie me to a chair an' tie my mouth up an' lock the do'—"

"And I comed over," said Jimmy eagerly, "and I run home and I see Mr. Algernon Jones is a robber and I phoned to Miss Minerva's beau, and if he'd brunged what I told him, he wouldn't never got cracked in the face like Mr. Algernon Jones done crack him, and Billy got to all time let robbers in the house so they can knock mans and little boys down."

"While you stand talking here the scoundrel will get away," said the injured man.

"That is so," agreed Doctor Sanford, "so I'll go and find the Sheriff."

Sarah Jane's huge form loomed up in the back-hall doorway, and she grabbed Jimmy by the arm.

"Yaas," she cried, "you gwine take you

a nap is yuh, yuh 'ceitful caterpillar. Come on home dis minute."

"Lemme go, Sarah Jane," protested the little boy, trying to jerk away from her; "I got to stay here and pertec' Billy and Miss Minerva's beau 'cause they's a robber might come back and tie 'em up and make 'em bleed if I ain't here."

"Did Mr. Algernon Jones make all that blood?" asked an awe-stricken little boy gazing in admiration at the victim of Mr. Jones's energy. "You sho' is a hero to stan' up an' let him knock you down like he done."

"Yes," cried Jimmy, as the black woman dragged him kicking and struggling through the hall, "we's all heroes, but I bet I'm the heroest hero they is, and I bet Miss Minerva's going to be mad 'bout you all spilling all that blood on her nice clean floor."

"Lemme see yo' big toe what was shot off

by all them Yankees and Injuns what you killed in the war," said Billy to Miss Minerva's beau.

The Major smiled at the little boy; a man-to-man smile, full of good comradeship, humor, and understanding. Billy's little heart went out to him at once.

"I can't take off my shoes at present," said the veteran. "Well, I must be going; I feel all right now."

Billy looked at him with big, solemn eyes.

"You couldn't never go 'thout yo' pants, could you?" he asked, "'cause Aunt Minerva jest nachelly despises pants."

The man eyed him quizzically.

"Well, no; I don't think I could," he replied; "I don't think I'd look any better in a Mother Hubbard or a kimono."

The little boy sighed.

"Which you think is the fittenest name," asked he, "Billy or William?"

"Billy, Billy," enthusiastically came the reply.

"I like mens," said William Green Hill. "I sho' wisht you could come and live right here with me and Aunt Minerva."

"I wish so, too," said the Major.

CHAPTER XV

BILLY, THE CREDULOUS

FTER the advent and disappearance of the exciting Mr. Jones, Miss Minerva, much to Billy's joy, had a telephone put in the house. He sat in the hall the day it was put in, waiting for it to ring.

Jimmy, coming up on the front porch and through the half-open door and seeing him sitting there, rang the door bell just for a joke, ready to burst into a laugh when the other little boy turned around and saw who it was. Billy, however, in his eagerness mistook the ring for the telephone bell and joyfully climbed up on the chair, which he had stationed in readiness. He took down the receiver as he had seen Jimmy do in his home and, without once seeing that little

163

boy standing a few feet from him, he yelled at the top of his lungs:

"Hello! Who is that?"

"This is Marie Yarbrough," replied Jimmy from the doorway, instantly recognizing Billy's mistake.

Marie Yarbrough was a little girl much admired by the two boys, as she had a pony and cart of her very own. However, she lived in a different part of the town and attended another Sunday school, so they had no speaking acquaintance with her.

"I jus' wanted to talk to you," went on the counterfeit Marie, stifling a laugh and trying to talk like a girl. "I think you're 'bout the sweetest little boy they is and I want you to come to my party."

"I sho' will," screamed the gratified Billy, "if Aunt Minerva 'll lemme. What make you talk so much like Jimmy?"

"Who?—that little old Jimmy Garner?

I hope I don't talk like that chicken; he's 'bout the measliest boy they is and I like you 'nother sight better'n him. You're a plumb jim-dandy, Billy," came from the doorway.

"So's you," howled back the delighted and flattered Billy.

Jimmy thought he would pop wide open in his efforts to keep from laughing.

"How'd you like to be my sweetheart?" he asked.

"I's already promise' to marry Miss Cecilia when I puts on long pants, but if we ever gits a 'vorse I'd 'nother sight ruther have you'n anybody. You can be my lady-frien', anyhow," was the loud reply.

"I'm coming for you to go riding in my little pony and cart," said a giggling Jimmy.

"All right, I's going to ask Aunt Minerva to lemme go. Can't we take Jimmy too?"

This was too much for the little boy. He

had held himself in as long as possible. He burst into a peal of laughter so merry and so loud that Billy, turning quickly, almost fell out of the chair.

"What you doin', a-listening to me talk to Marie Yarbrough th'oo the telephone?" he questioned angrily.

"Marie your pig's foot," was the inelegant response. "That was just me a-talking to you all the time. You all time think you talking to little girls and all time 'taint nobody but me."

A light dawned upon the innocent one. He promptly hung up the receiver and got down out of the chair. Before Jimmy was fully aware of his intention, Billy had thrown him to the floor and was giving him a good pommeling.

"Say you got 'nough?" he growled from his position astride of the other boy.

"I got 'nough," repeated Jimmy.

"Say you sorry you done it."

"I say I sorry I done it," abjectly repeated the younger child. "Get up, Billy, 'fore you bust my stommick open."

"Say you ain't never a-goin' to tell no-

body, cross yo' heart," he commanded next.

"I say I ain't never going to tell nobody, cross my heart. Get up, Billy, 'fore you made me mad, and ain't no telling what I'll do to you if I get mad."

"Say you's a low-down Jezebel skunk."

"I ain't going to say I'm nothing of the kind," spiritedly replied the under-dog. "You all time wanting somebody to call theirselfs someping. You're a low-down Isabella skunk yourself."

"You got to say it," insisted the victor, renewing hostilities.

"I'll say I'm a Isabella 'cause Isabella discovered America and 's in the Bible," replied the tormented one; "Miss Cecilia 'splained it to me."

Billy accepted his compromise and Jimmy's flattened stomach, relieved of its burden, puffed out to its usual roundness as that little boy rose to his feet, saying:

"Sam Lamb would 'a' died a-laughing, Billy, if he'd seen you telephoning."

"He'd better never hear tell of it," was the threatening rejoinder.

CHAPTER XVI

THE HUMBLE PETITION

ILLY, sitting in an old buggy in front of the livery stable, had just engaged in a long and interesting conversation with Sam Lamb. He was getting out of the vehicle when the sharp wire around a broken rod caught in the back of his trousers and tore a great hole. He felt a tingling pain and looked over his shoulder to investigate. Not being satisfied with the result, he turned his back to the negro and anxiously enquired, "Is my breeches tore, Sam?"

"Dey am dat," was the reply; "dey am busted f'm Dan ter Beersheba."

"What I goin' to do 'bout it?" asked the little boy. "Aunt Minerva sho' will be mad. These here's bran-spankin' new trou-

sers what I ain't never wore tell to-day.
Ain't you got a needle an' thread so's you
can fix 'em, Sam?"

"Nary er needle," said Sam Lamb.

"Is my union suit tore, too?" and Billy
again turned his back for inspection.

His friend made a close examination.

"Yo' unions is injured plum scanerlous,"
was his discouraging decision, "and hit
'pears ter me dat yo' hide done suffer too;
you's got er turrible scratch."

The child sighed. The injury to the flesh
was of small importance,—he could hide
that from his aunt—but the rent in his
trousers was a serious matter.

"I wish I could git 'em mended 'fore I
goes home," he said wistfully.

"I tell you what do," suggested Sam; "I
'low Miss Cecilia'll holp yeh; jest go by her
house an' she'll darn 'em up fer yuh."

Billy hesitated.

"Well, you see, Sam, me an' Miss Cecilia's engaged an' we's fixin' to marry jes' 's soon's I puts on long pants, an' I 'shame' to ask her. An' I don't berlieve young 'omans patches the breeches of young mans what they's goin' to marry nohow. Do

you? Aunt Minerva ain' never patched no breeches for the Major. And then," with a modest blush, "my unions is tore too, an' I ain't got on nothin' else to hide my skin."

Again he turned his back to his friend and, his clouded little face looking over his shoulder, he asked, "Do my meat show, Sam?"

"She am visible ter de naked eye!"

"I don't believe God pays me much attention nohow," said the little boy dolefully; "ev'y day I gets put to bed 'cause somepin's all time a-happenin'. If He'd had a eye on me like He oughter they wouldn't 'a' been no snaggin'. Aunt Minerva's goin' to be mad th'oo an' th'oo."

"Maybe my ol' 'oman can fix em, so's dey won't be so turrible bad," suggested the negro. "'T ain't fur, so you jes' run down ter my cabin an' tell Sukey I say fix dem breeches."

The child needed no second bidding, — he
fairly flew. Sam's wife was cooking, but
she cheerfully stopped her work to help the
little boy. She sewed up his union suit and
put a bright blue patch on his brown linen
breeches.

Billy felt a little more cheerful, though he
still dreaded confessing to his aunt and he
loitered along the way till it was nearly
dark. Supper was ready when he got home
and he walked into the dining-room with his
customary ease and grace. But he took his
seat uneasily, and he was so quiet during the
meal and ate so little that his aunt asked him
if he were sick. He was planning in his
mind how to break the news of the day's dis-
aster to her.

"You are improving, William," she remarked presently; "you haven't got into any
mischief to-day. You have been a mighty
good little boy now for two days."

Billy flushed at the compliment and shifted uneasily in his seat. That patch seemed to burn him.

"If God'd just do His part," he said darkly, "I wouldn't never git in no meanness."

After supper Miss Minerva washed the dishes in the kitchen sink and Billy carried them back to the dining-room. His aunt caught him several times prancing sideways in the most idiotic manner. He was making a valiant effort to keep from exposing his rear elevation to her; once he had to walk backward.

"William," she said sharply, "you will break my plates. What is the matter with you to-night?"

A little later they were sitting quietly in Miss Minerva's room. She was reading "The Christian at Home," and he was absently looking at a picture book.

"Sam Lamb's wife Sukey sho' is a beautiful patcher," he remarked, feeling his way.

She made no answering comment, and the discouraged little boy was silent for a few minutes. He had worn Aunt Cindy's many-colored patches too often to be ashamed of this one for himself, but he felt that he would like to draw his aunt out and find how she stood on the subject of patches.

"Aunt Minerva," he presently asked, "what sorter patches'd you ruther wear on yo' pants, blue patches or brown?"

"On my what?" she asked, looking at him severely over her paper.

"I mean if you's me," he hastily explained. "Don't you think blue patches is the mos' nat'ral lookin'?"

"What are you driving at, William?" she asked; but without waiting for his answer she went on with her reading.

The child was silent for a long time, his

little mind busy, then he began, "Aunt Minerva—"

She peered at him over her glasses a second, then dropped her eyes to the paper where an interesting article on Foreign Missions held her attention.

"Aunt Minerva, I snagged—Aunt Minerva, I snagged my—my skin, to-day."

"Let me see the place," she said absently, her eyes glued to a paragraph describing a cannibal feast.

"I's a-settin' on it right now," he replied.

Another long silence ensued. Billy resolved to settle the matter.

"I's gettin' sleepy," he yawned. "Aunt Minerva, I wants to say my prayers and go to bed."

She laid her paper down and he dropped to his knees by her side. He usually sprawled all over her lap during his lengthy devotions, but to-night he clasped his little hands and reared back like a rabbit on its haunches.

After he had rapidly repeated the Lord's prayer, which he had recently learned, and had invoked blessings on all his new friends and never-to-be-forgotten old ones, he con-cluded with:

"An', O Lord, You done kep' me f'om meddlin' with Aunt Minerva's hose any mo', an' you done kep' me f'om gittin' any mo' Easter eggs, an' playin' any mo' Injun, an' You done kep' me f'om lettin' Mr. Algernon Jones come ag'in, an' now, O Lord, please don't lemme worry the very 'zistence outer Aunt Minerva any mo'n You can help, like she said I done this mornin', an' please, if Thy will be done, don't lemme tear the next new breeches what she'll gimme like I done ruint these here what I got on."

CHAPTER XVII

A GREEN-EYED BILLY

AVE some candy?" said Miss Cecilia, offering a big box of bonbons to Billy, who was visiting her.

"Where'd you git 'em?" he asked, as he helped himself generously.

"Maurice sent them to me this morning."

Billy put all his candy back into the box.

"I don't believe I wants noner yo' candy," he said, scowling darkly. "I reckon you likes him better'n me anyhow, don't you?"

"I love you dearly," she replied.

The child stood in front of her and looked her squarely in the eye. His little form was drawn to its full, proud height, his soft fair cheeks were flushed, his big, beautiful, gray eyes looked sombre and sad.

"Is you in love with that red-headed Maurice Richmond an' jes' a-foolin' o' me?"

A bright flush dyed crimson the young lady's pretty face.

She put her arm around the childish, graceful figure and drew the little boy to the sofa beside her.

"Now, honey, you mustn't be silly," she said gently; "you are my own dear little sweetheart."

"An' I reckon he's yo' own, dear, big sweetheart," said the jealous Billy. "Well, all I got to say is this-here: if he's a-goin' to come to see you ev'y day, then I ain't never comin' no mo'. He's been a-carryin' on his foolishness 'bout 's long as I can stand it. You got to chose 'tween us right this minute; he come down here mos' ev'y day; he's tuck you drivin' more 'n fifty hunderd times, an' he's give you all the candy you can stuff."

"He is not the only one who comes to see me," she said smiling down at him. "Jimmy comes often and Len Hammer and Will Reid. Don't you want them to come?"

"Don't nobody pay no 'tention to Jimmy," he replied contemptuously; "he ain't nothing' but a baby, an' them other mens can come if you wants 'em to; but," said Billy, with a lover's unerring intuition, "I ain't a-goin' to stand fer that long-legged, sorrel-top Maurice Richmond a-trottin' his great big carkiss down here ev'y minute. I wish Aunt Minerva'd let me put on long pants to-morrer so's we could git married." He caught sight of a new ring sparkling on her finger.

"Who give you that ring?"

"A little bird brought it to me," she said, trying to speak gayly, and blushing again.

"A big, red-headed peckerwood," said Billy savagely.

"Maurice loves you, too,"—she hoped to conciliate him; "he says you are the brightest kid in town."

"Kid," was the scornful echo. "'Cause he's so big and tall, he's got to call me a kid. Well, he's jes' a-wastin' hisself lovin' me; I don't like him an' I ain't a-goin' to never like him an' soon's I puts on long pants he's goin' to get 'bout the worses' lickin' he ever did see.

"Say, does you kiss him like you does me?" he asked presently, looking up at her with serious, unsmiling face.

She hid her embarrassment in a laugh.

"Don't be foolish, Billy," she replied.

"I'll bet he's kissed you more 'n fifty hunderd times."

"There's Jimmy whistling for you," said Miss Cecilia. "How do you two boys make that peculiar whistle? I would recognize it anywhere."

"Is he ever kiss you yet?" asked the child.

"I heard that you and Jimmy whipped Ed Brown because he imitated your own particular whistle. Did you?"

"How many times is he kiss you?" asked Billy.

The young girl put her arm around him and tried to nestle his little body against her own.

"I'm too big, anyway, for your real sweetheart," she said. "Why, by the time you are large enough to marry I should be an old maid. You must have Frances or Lina for your sweetheart."

"An' let you have Maurice!" he sneered.

She stooped to lay her flushed cheek against his own.

"Honey," she softly said, "Maurice and I are going to be married soon; I love him very much and I want you to love him too."

He pushed her roughly from him.

"An' you jes' 'ceived me all the time," he cried, "an' me a-lovin' you better'n anybody I ever see sence I's born? An' you a Sunday-school teacher! I ain't never a-goin' to trus' nobody no mo'. Good-bye, Miss Cecilia."

She caught his hand and held it fast. "I want you and Jimmy to be my little pages at the wedding, and wear dear little white satin suits all trimmed with gold braid,"— she tried to be enthusiastic and arouse his interest; "and Lina and Frances can be little flowergirls and we'll have such a beautiful wedding."

"Jimmy an' Lina an' Frances can be all the pages an' flower-girls an' brides an' grooms they wants to, but you can't rope me in," he scornfully replied. "I's done with you an' I ain't never goin' to have me no mo' sweetheart long's I live."

CHAPTER XVIII

CLOSER THAN A BROTHER

T was a bad, rainy day. Jimmy and Billy were playing in Sarah Jane's cabin, she, however, being in happy ignorance of the fact. Her large stays, worn to the preaching the night before, were hanging on the back of a chair.

"Ain't I glad I don' have to wear no corset when I puts on long pants?" remarked Billy, pointing to the article. "Ain't that a big one? It's twice big's Aunt Minerva's."

"My mama wears a big co'set, too," said Jimmy; "I like fat womans 'nother sight better'n lean ones. Miss Minerva's 'bout the skinniest woman they is; when I get married I'm going to pick me out the fattest wife I can find, so when you set in her lap at night

for her to rock you to sleep you'll have a soft
place to put your head, while she sings to
you."

"The Major—he's mos' plump enough
for two," said Billy, taking down the stays
and trying to hook them around him.

"It sho' is big," he said; "I berlieve it's
'most big 'nough to go way 'round the both
of us."

"Le's see if 'tain't," was the other boy's
ready suggestion.

He stood behind Billy and they put the
stays around both little bodies, while, with
much squeezing and giggling, Billy hooked
them safely up the front. The boys got in
front of Sarah Jane's one looking-glass and
danced about laughing with glee.

"We're like the twinses what was growed
together like mama read me 'bout," declared
the younger child.

Presently they began to feel uncomfort-

able, especially Jimmy, whose fat, round little middle was tightly compressed.

"Here, unhook this thing, Billy, and le's
take her off," he said. "I'm 'bout to pop
open."

"All right," agreed his companion.

He tugged and pulled, but could get only
the top and bottom hooks unclasped; the
middle ones refused to budge.

"I can't get these-here hooks to come
loose," Billy said.

Jimmy put his short, fat arms around him
and tried his hand, but with no better success. The stays were such a snug fit that
the hooks seemed glued.

"We sho' is in a fix," said Billy gloomily;
"look like God all time lettin' us git in
trouble."

"You think of more fool stunts to do,
William Hill, than any boy they is," cried
the other; "you all time want to get us

hooked up in Sarah Jane's corset and you all time can't get nobody loose. What you want to get us hooked up in this thing for?"

"You done it yo'self," defended the boy in front with rising passion. "Squeeze in, Jimmy; we jes' boun' to git outer this 'fore somebody finds it out."

He backed the other child close to the wall and pressed so hard against him that Jimmy screamed aloud and began to pound him on the head with his chubby fists.

Billy would not submit tamely to any such treatment. He reached his hand behind him and gave the smaller boy's cheek a merciless pinch. The fight was on. The two little boys, laced up tightly as they were in a stout pair of stays, pinched and scratched, and kicked and jerked. Suddenly Billy, leaning heavily against Jimmy, threw him flat on his back and fell on top of him.

Bennie Dick, sitting on the floor, had up

to this time watched the proceedings with an interested eye; now, thinking murder was being committed, he opened his big, red mouth and emitted a howl that could be heard half a mile. It immediately brought his mother to the open door. When she saw

A. MAC. D.

the children squirming on the floor in her only corset, her indignation knew no bounds.

"You, Jimmy Garner, an' you, too, William Hill, yuh little imps o' Satan, what you doin' in my house? Didn't yo' mammy tell you not to tamper wid me no mo'? Git up an' come here an' lemme git my co'set off o' yuh."

Angry as she was she could not keep from laughing at the sight they presented, as, with no gentle hand, she unclasped the hooks and released their imprisoned bodies.

"Billy all time—" began Jimmy.

"Billy all time nothin'," said Sarah Jane. "'T ain't no use fo' to try to lay dis-here co'set business onto Billy; both o' yuh is ekally in it. An' me a-aimin' fo' to go to three fun'els dis week an' a baptizin' on Sunday. S'pose y' all 'd bruck one o' de splints, how'd I look a-presidin' at a fun'el 'thout nare co'set on, an' me shape' like what I is?"

"Who's dead, Sarah Jane?" asked Jimmy, interestedly, hoping to stem the torrent of her wrath.

"Sis' Mary Ellen's las' husban', Brudder Littlejohn—dat's a-who," she replied, somewhat mollified at his interest.

"When did he die?" said Jimmy, pursuing his advantage.

"He got 'way f'om here 'bout moon-down las' night," she replied, losing sight of her grievance in his flattering interrogations. "You know Sis' Littlejohn; she been married goin' on five times. Dis-here'll make fo' gentlemans she done buriet an' dey ain't nobody can manage a fun'el like she kin; 'pears like hit jes' come natchel to her. She sho' is done a good part by eb'ry single husban' too, an' she's figgerin' to outdo all the yuthers wid Brudder Littlejohn's co'pse." Sarah Jane almost forgot her little audience in her intense absorption of her subject. "She say to me dis mornin', she say, 'Marri'ge am a lott'ry, Sis Beddinfiel', but I sho' is drawed some han'some prizes.' She got 'em all laid out side by side in de buryin' groun' wid er little imige on ebry grabe; an' Sis Mary Ellen, seein' as she can't read de

writin' on de tombstones, she got a diff'unt
little animal a-settin' on eb'ry head res' so's
she kin tell which husban' am which. Her
fus' husban' were all time a-huntin', so she
got a little white marble pa'tridge a-restin'
on he head, an' hit am a mighty console-
ment to a po' widda 'oman fo' to know dat
she can tell de very minute her eyes light
on er grabe which husban' hit am. Her
secon' man he got er mighty kinky, woolly
head an' he mighty meek, so she got a little
white lamb a-settin' on he grabe; an' de nex'
husban' he didn't have nothin' much fo' to
disgueese him f'om de res' 'cep'in he so slow
an' she might'nigh rack her brain off, twell
she happen to think 'bout him bein' a Hard-
shell Baptis' an' so powerful slow, so she jes
got a little terrapim an' sot it on him. Hit
sho' am a pretty sight jes' to go in dat buryin' groun' an' look at 'em all, side by side;
an' now she got Brudder Littlejohn to add

to de res'. He de onliest one what's got er patch o' whiskers so she gwine to put a little white cat on he grabe. Yes, Lord, ef any-think could pearten a widda 'oman hit would be jes' to know dat yuh could go to de grabeyard any time yuh want to an' look at dat han'some c'llection an' tell 'zactly which am which."

Sarah Jane stopped for breath and Billy hastened to inquire.

"Who else is dead, Sarah Jane?"

"'T ain't nobody else dead, yit, as I knows on, but my two cousins is turrible low; one's got a hem'rage on de lung an' de yuther's got a congesti'n on de brain, an' I 'lows dey'll bofe drap off 'twix' now an' sun-up to-morra." Her eyes rolled around and happened to light on her corset. She at once returned to her grievance.

"An' sposin' I hadn't 'a' came in here when I did? I'd 'a' had to went to my own cousins' fun'el 'thout nare co'set. Y'all gotta go right to y'all's mama an' Miss Minerva dis very minute. I low dey'll settle yo' hashes. Don't y'all know dat Larroes ketch meddlers?"

CHAPTER XIX

TWINS AND A SISSY

RS. HAMILTON and Mrs. Black were sitting on Miss Minerva's veranda talking to her, and Lina and Frances were in the swing with Billy.

The attraction proved too great for Jimmy; he impolitely left a disconsolate little visitor sitting on his own porch while he jumped the fence and joined the other children.

"Don't you all wish you could see Mrs. Brown's new twinses?" was his greeting as he took his seat by Billy.

"Where'd she get 'em?" asked Frances.

"Doctor Sanford tooken 'em to her last night."

"He muster found 'em in a holler stump,"

remarked Billy. "I knows, 'cause that's where Doctor Shacklefoot finds aller ol' Aunt Blue-Gum Tempy's Peruny Pearline's, an' me an' Wilkes Booth Lincoln been lookin' in ev'y holler stump we see ever sence we's born, an' we ain't never foun' no baby 't all, 'cause can't nobody but jes' doctors fin' 'em. I wish he'd a-give 'em to Aunt Minerva 'stidder Mrs. Brown."

"I wish he'd bringed 'em to my mama," said Frances.

"I certainly do think he might have given them to us," declared Lina, "and I'm going to tell him so, too. As much money as father has paid him for doctor's bills and as much old, mean medicine as I have taken just to 'commodate him; then he gives babies to everybody but us."

"I'm awfully glad he never give 'em to my mama," said Jimmy, "'cause I never could had no more fun; they'd be stuck right under

my nose all time, and all time put their
mouth in everything you want to do, and all
time meddling. You can't fool me 'bout
twinses. But I wish I could see 'em! They
so weakly they got to be hatched in a
nincubator."

"What's that?" questioned Frances.

"That's a someping what you hatches
chickens and babies in when they's delicate,
and ain't got 'nough breath and ain't got
they eyes open and ain't got no feathers on,"
explained Jimmy.

"Reckon we can see 'em?" she asked.

"See nothing!" sniffed the little boy.
"Ever sence Billy let Mr. Algernon Jones
whack Miss Minerva's beau we can't do
nothing a-tall 'thout grown folks 'r' stuck
right under your nose. I'm jes cramped to
death."

"When I'm a mama," mused Frances, "I
hope Doctor Sanford'll bring me three little

twinses, and two Maltese kittens, and a little Japanee, and a monkey, and a parrit."

"When I'm a papa," said Jimmy, "I don' want no babies a-tall; all they's good for is jus' to set 'round and yell."

"Look like God'd sho' be busy a-makin' so many babies," remarked Billy.

"Why, God don' have none o' the trouble," explained Jimmy. "He's just got Him a baby factory in Heaven like the chair factory and the canning factory down by the railroad, and angels jus' all time make they arms and legs, like niggers do at the chair factory, and all God got to do is jus' glue 'em together, and stick in their souls. God's got 'bout the easiest job they is."

"I thought angels jes' clam' the golden stair and play they harps," said Billy.

"Ain't we going to look sweet at Miss Cecilia's wedding?" said Frances, after a short silence.

"I'll betcher I'll be the cutest kid in that church," boasted Jimmy conceitedly. "You coming, ain't you, Billy?"

"I gotter go," answered that jilted swain, gloomily; "Aunt Minerva ain't got nobody to leave me with at home. I jes' wish she'd git married."

"Why wouldn't you be a page, Billy?" asked Lina.

"'Cause I didn't hafto," he snapped.

"I bet my mama give her the finest present they is," bragged the smaller boy; "I reckon it cost 'bout a million dollars."

"Mother gave her a handsome cut-glass vase," said Lina.

"It looks like Doctor Sanford would've give Miss Cecilia those twinses for a wedding present," said Frances.

"Who is that little boy sitting on your porch, Jimmy?" asked Lina, noticing for the first time a lonely-looking child.

"That's Leon Tipton, Aunt Ella's little boy. He just come out from Memphis to spend the day with me and I'll be awful glad when he goes home; he's 'bout the stuck-up-est kid they is, and skeery? He's 'bout the 'fraidest young un ever you see. And look at him now? Wears long curls like a girl and don't want to never get his clean clo'es dirty."

"I think he's a beautiful little boy," championed Lina. "Call him over here, Jimmy."

"Naw, I don't want to. You all'll like him a heap better over there; he's one o' these-here kids what the furder you get 'way from 'em, the better you like 'em."

"He sho' do look lonesome," said Billy; "'vite him over, Jimmy."

"Leon!" screamed his cousin, "you can come over here if you wantta."

The lonesome-looking little boy promptly accepted the invitation, and came primly

through the two gates. He walked proudly
to the swing and stood, cap in hand, waiting
for an introduction.

"Why didn't you clam' the fence, 'stead
of coming th'oo the gates?" growled Jimmy.
"You 'bout the prissiest boy they is. Well,
why don't you set down?"

"Introduce me, please," said the elegant
little city boy.

"Interduce your grandma's pussy cats,"
mocked Jimmy. "Set down, I tell you."

Frances and Lina made room for him between them and soon gave him their undivided attention, to the intense envy and
disgust of the other two little boys.

"I am Lina Hamilton," said the little girl
on his right.

"And I'm Frances Black, and Jimmy
ought to be 'shamed to treat you like he
does."

"I knows a turrible skeery tale," remarked

a malicious Billy, looking at Lina and Frances. "If y' all wa'n't girls I'd tell it to you."

"We aren't any more scared'n you, William Hill," cried Frances, her interest at once aroused; "I already know 'bout 'raw meat and bloody bones' and nothing's scarier'n that."

"And I know 'Fe, Fi, Fo, Fum, I smell the blood of an Englishman. Be he alive or be he dead, I'll ground his bones to make me bread,'" said Lina.

"This-here tale," continued Billy, glueing his big eyes to those of the little stranger, "is one Tabernicle learnt fer a speech at school. It's all 'bout a 'oman what was buriet in a graveyard with a diamant ring on her finger, an' a robber come in the night—" The child's tones were guttural, thrilling, and hair-raising as he glared into the eyes of the effeminate Leon—"an' a robber come in the night an' try to cut it off, an' ha'nts was groanin' an' the win' moan 'oo-oo' an' —"

Leon could stand it no longer.

"I am going right back," he cried, rising with round, frightened eyes; "I am not going to sit here and listen to you, scaring little girls to death. You are a bad boy to scare Lina and Frances and I am not going to associate with you!", and this champion of the fair sex stalked with dignity across the yard to the gate.

"I'm no more scared'n nothing," an indignant Frances hurled at his back. "You're just scared yourself."

Jimmy giggled happily. "What'd I tell you all," he cried, gleefully. "Lina and Frances got to all time set little 'fraid cats 'tween 'em," he snorted. "It's just like I tell you, he's the sissiest boy they is; and he don't care who kiss him neither; he'll let

any woman kiss him what wants to. Can't
no woman at all 'cepting my mama and Miss
Cecilia kiss me. But Leon is 'bout the
kissingest kid they is; why, he'd just as
soon's not let Frances and Lina kiss him;
he ain't got no better sense. Course I gotta
let Miss Cecilia kiss me 'cause she's 'bout
the plumpest Sunday-school teacher they
is and the Bible say 'If your Sunday-school
teacher kiss you on one cheek, turn the other
cheek and let her kiss you on that, too,' and
I all time bound to do what the Bible say.
You'd better call him back, Frances, and
kiss him, you and Lina're so stuck on him."

"I wouldn't kiss him to save his life,"
declared Frances; "he's got the spindliest
legs I ever saw."

CHAPTER XX

RISING IN THE WORLD

HE painter had just finished putting a bright green coat of paint upon the low, flat roof of Miss Minerva's long back-porch. And he left his ladder leaning against the house while he went inside to confer with Miss Minerva in regard to some other work.

Billy, Jimmy, Frances, and Lina had been playing "Fox and Geese." Running around the house they spied the ladder and saw no owner to deny them.

"Le's clam' up and get on top the porch," suggested Jimmy.

"Aunt Minerva'll put me to bed if I do," said Billy.

"Mother'll make me learn a whole page

of the catechism if I climb a ladder," said Lina.

"My mama'll shut me up in the closet, but our mamas aren't bound to know 'bout it," —this from Frances. "Come on, let's climb up."

"I ain't never promise not to clam' no ladder, but—" Billy hesitated.

"You-all 'bout the skeeriest folks they is," sneered Jimmy. "Mama'll whip me going, and coming if she finds out 'bout it, but I ain't skeered. I dare anybody to dare me to clam' up."

"I dare you to climb this ladder," responded an accommodating Frances.

"I ain't never tooken a dare yet," boasted the little boy proudly, his foot on the bottom rung. "Who's going to foller me?"

"Don't we have fun?" cried a jubilant Frances.

"Yes," answered Jimmy; "if grown folks

don't all time be watching you and sticking theirselfs in your way."

"If people would let us alone," remarked Lina, "we could enjoy ourselves every day."

"But grown folks got to be so pertic'lar with you all time," cried Jimmy; "they don't never want us to play together."

He led the way up the ladder, followed by Frances and Billy; and Lina brought up the rear. The children ran the long length of the porch, leaving their footprints on the fresh, sticky paint.

"Will it wash off?" asked Frances, looking gloomily down at her feet, which seemed to be encased in green moccasins.

At that moment she slipped and fell sprawling on top of the roof. When the others helped her to her feet, she was a sight to behold, her white dress splotched with vivid green from top to bottom.

"If that ain't jus' like you, Frances," Jimmy exclaimed; "you all time got to fall down and get paint on your dress so we can't 'ceive nobody. Now our mamas bound to know 'bout us clamming up here."

"They would know it anyhow," mourned Lina; "we'll never get this paint off of our feet. We had better get right down and see if we can't wash some of it off."

While they were talking the owner of the ladder, who had not noticed them—and was deaf in the bargain—had quietly removed it from the back-porch and carried it around to the front of the house.

The children looked at each other in consternation when they perceived their loss.

"What we goin' to do now?" asked Billy.

"If this ain't just like Billy, all time got to perpose to clam' a ladder and all time got to let the ladder get loose from him," growled Jimmy. "We done cooked a goose egg, this time. You got us up here, Billy; how you going to get us down?"

"I didn't, neither."

"Well, it's Miss Minerva's house and she's your aunt and we's your company and you got to be 'sponsible."

"I can clam' down this-here post," said the responsible party.

"I can climb down it, too," seconded Frances.

"You can't clam' down nothing at all," said Jimmy contemptuously. "Talk 'bout you can clam' down a post; you'd fall and bust yourself wide open; you 'bout the clumsiest girl there is; 'sides, your legs're too fat."

"We can holler," was Lina's suggestion.

"And have grown folks laughing fit to pop their sides open? I'm 'shame' to go anywheres now 'cause folks all time telling me when I'm going to dye some more Easter eggs! Naw, we better not holler," said Jimmy. "Ain't you going to do nothing, Billy?"

"I'll jest slide down this-here post and git the painter man to bring his ladder back. Y'all wait up here."

Billy's solution of the difficulty seemed the safest, and they were soon released from their elevated prison.

"I might as well go home and be learning the catechism," groaned Lina.

"I'm goin to get right in 'the closet soon's I get to my house," said Frances. "Go on and put on your night-shirt, Billy."

Billy took himself to the bathroom and scrubbed and scrubbed; but the paint refused to come off. He tiptoed by the kitchen where his aunt was cooking dinner and ran into his own room.

He found the shoes and stockings which were reserved for Sunday wear, and soon had them upon his little feet.

Miss Minerva rang the dinner-bell and he walked quietly into the dining-room trying to make as little noise and to attract as little attention from his aunt as possible; but she fastened her eyes at once upon his feet.

"What are you doing with your shoes on, William?" she asked.

Billy glanced nonchalantly at her.

"Don't you think, Aunt Minerva," he made answer, "I's gittin' too big to go 'thout any shoes? I's mos' ready to put on long pants, an' how'd I look, I'd jest like to know, goin' roun' barefooted an' got on long breeches. I don' believe I'll go barefooted no mo' — I'll jest wear my shoes ev'y day."

"I just believe you won't. Go take them off at once and hurry back to your dinner."

"Lemme jest wait till I eats," he begged, hoping to postpone the evil hour of exposure.

"No, go at once, and be sure and wash your hands."

Miss Minerva spied the paint the instant he made his second entrance and immediately inquired, "How did you get that paint on your feet?"

The little boy took his seat at the table

and looked up at her with his sweet, attractive, winning smile.

"Paint pertec's little boys' feets," he said,
"an' keeps 'em from gittin' hurted, Aunt
Minerva, don't it?"

Miss Minerva laid down her fork and
gave her nephew her undivided attention.

"You have been getting into mischief
again, I see, William; now tell me all about
it. Are you afraid of me?"

"Yas'm," was his prompt response, "an'
I don't want to be put to bed neither. The
Major he wouldn't put little boys to bed
daytimes."

She blushed and eyed him thoughtfully.
She was making slow progress with the
child, she knew, yet she still felt it her stern
duty to be very strict with him and, having
laid down certain rules to rear him by, she
wished to adhere to them.

"William," she said after he had made a

full confession, "I won't punish you this
time, for I know that Jimmy led you into it,
but—"

"Naw'm, Jimmy didn't. Me an' him an'
Frances an Lina's all 'sponsible, but I
promise you, Aunt Minerva, not to clam' no
mo' ladders."

CHAPTER XXI

PRETENDING REALITY

THE chain-gang had been work-ing in the street not far from Miss Minerva's house, and Lina, Frances, Billy and Jimmy had hung on her front fence for an hour, watching them with eager interest. The negroes were chained together in pairs, and guarded by two, big, burly white men.

"Let's us play chain-gang," suggested Jimmy.

"Where we goin' to git a chain?" queried Billy; "'twon't be no fun 'thout a lock an' chain."

"I can get the lock and chain off'm Sarah Jane's cabin."

"Yo' mama don't 'low you to go to her cabin," said Billy.

"My mama don't care if I just borra a lock and chain; so I'm going to get it."

"I'm going to be the perlice of the gang," said Frances.

"Perlice nothing. You all time talking 'bout you going to be the perlice," scoffed Jimmy. "I'm going to be the perlice myself."

"No, you are not," interposed Lina, firmly. "Billy and I are the tallest and we are going to be the guards, and you and Frances must be the prisoners."

"Well, I ain't going to play 'thout I can be the boss of the niggers. It's Sarah Jane's chain and she's my mama's cook, and I'm going to be what I please."

"I'll tell you what do," was Billy's suggestion; "we'll take it turn about; me an' Lina'll firs' be the perlice an' y'all be the chain-gang, an' then we'll be the niggers an' y'all be the bosses."

This arrangement was satisfactory, so the younger boy climbed the fence and soon returned with a short chain and padlock.

Billy chained Jimmy and Frances together by two round, fat ankles and put the key to the lock in his pocket.

"We must decide what crimes they have committed," said Lina.

"Frances done got 'rested fer shootin' craps an' Jimmy done got 'rested fer 'sturbin' public worship," said the other boss.

"Naw I ain't, neither," objected the male member of the chain-gang; "I done cut my woman with a razor 'cause I see her racking down the street like a proud coon with another gent, like what Sarah Jane's brother told me he done at the picnic."

The children played happily together for half an hour, Billy and Lina commanding and the prisoners, entering thoroughly into the spirit of the game, according prompt obedience to their bosses. At last the captives wearied of their role and clamored for an exchange of parts.

"All right," agreed Lina. "Get the key, Billy, and we'll be the chain-gang."

Billy put his right hand in his pocket but found no key there; he tried the other pocket with the same success; he felt in his blouse, he looked in his cap, he jumped up and down, he nearly shook himself to pieces, all without avail; the key had disappeared as if by magic.

"I berlieve y' all done los' that key," concluded he.

"Maybe it dropped on the ground," said Frances.

They searched the yard over, but the key was not to be found.

"Well, if that ain't just like you, Billy," cried Jimmy; "you all time perposing to play chain-gang and you all time lose the key."

Lina grew indignant.

"You proposed this yourself, Jimmy Garner," she said; "we never would have thought of playing chain-gang but for you."

"It looks like we can't never do anything at all," mourned Frances, "'thout grown folks've got to know 'bout it."

"Yes, and laugh fit to pop theirselfs open," said her fellow-prisoner. "I can't never pass by Owen Gibbs and Len Hammer now 'thout they laugh just like idjets and grin just like pole-cats."

"I ain't never hear tell of a pole-cat grinnin'," corrected Billy; "he jest all time smell worser 'n what a billy goat do."

"It is Chessy cats that grin," explained Lina.

"Look like folks would get 'em a lot of pole-cats stead o' chillens always hafto be

wearing assfetty bags 'round their nakes,
so's they can keep off whopping-cough,"
said Frances.

"You can't wear a pole-cat 'roun' yo'
nake," grinned Billy.

"And Len Hammer all time now asking
me," Jimmy continued, "when I'm going to
wear Sarah Jane's co'set to Sunday school.

Grown folks 'bout the lunatickest things they is. Ain't you going to unlock this chain, Billy?" he demanded.

"What I got to unlock it with?" asked Billy.

As Jimmy's father was taking the crestfallen chain-gang to the blacksmith shop to have their fetters removed, they had to pass by the livery stable; and Sam Lamb, bent double with intoxicating mirth at their predicament, yelled:

"Lordee! Lordee! Y' all sho' is de outlandishest kids 'twixt de Bad Place an' de moon."

CHAPTER XXII

A TRANSACTION IN MUMPS

"ON'T you come near me," screamed Billy, sauntering slowly and deliberately toward the dividing fence; "keep 'way f'om me; they's ketchin'."

Jimmy was sitting on his front steps and the proverbial red flag could not have excited a bull to quicker action. He hopped down the steps and ran across his own yard toward Billy as fast as his short, fat legs could carry him.

"Git 'way f'om me; you'll ketch 'em if you teches me," warned Billy; "an' you too little to have 'em," and he waved an authoritative hand at the other child. But Jimmy's curiosity was aroused to the highest pitch. He promptly jumped the fence and gazed at the bandaged face of his chum with critical admiration.

"What's the matter?" he inquired. "You got the toothache?"

"Toothache!" was the scornful echo, "well, I reckon not. Git back; don't you tech 'em; you ain't ol' 'nough to have 'em."

Billy's head was swathed in a huge, white cloth; his usually lean little cheeks were puffed out till he resembled a young hippopotamus, and his pretty gray eyes were almost invisible.

"You better git 'way f'om me an' don't tech 'em, like I tells you," he reiterated. "Aunt Minerva say you ain't never had 'em an' she say fer me to make you keep 'way f'om me 'cause you ain't a ol' chile like what I is."

"You ain't but six," retorted angry Jimmy, "and I'll be six next month; you all time trying to 'suade little boys to think

you're 'bout a million years old. What's
the matter with you, anyhow? You 'bout
the funniest looking kid they is."

Billy theatrically touched a distended
cheek. "These here is mumps," he said
impressively; "an' when you got 'em you
can make grown folks do perzactly what
you want 'em to. Aunt Minerva's in the
kitchen right now makin' me a 'lasses custard if I'll be good an' stay right in the house
an' don't come out here in the yard an' don't
give you the mumps. Course I can't tech
that custard now 'cause I done come out
here an' it ain't hon'r'ble; but she's makin'
it jes' the same. You better git 'way f'om
me an' not tech 'em; you too little to have
'em."

"Are they easy to ketch?" asked the other
little boy eagerly; "lemme jest tech 'em one
time, Billy."

"Git 'way, I tell you," warned the latter

with a superior air. To increase Jimmy's envy he continued: "Grown folks tries to see how nice they can be to chillens what's got the mumps. Aunt Minerva ain't been impedent to me to-day; she lemme do jest 'bout like I please; it sho' is one time you can make grown folks step lively." He looked at Jimmy meditatively, "It sho' is a plumb pity you ain't a ol' chile like what I is an' can't have the mumps. Yo' ma'd be skeered to spank you, skeered she'd injuh yo' mumps. Don't you come any closter to me," he again warned; "you too little to have 'em."

"I'll give you five peewees if you'll lemme tech 'em so's I can get 'em," pleaded the younger boy.

Billy hesitated. "You mighty little—" he began.

"And my stoney," said the other child eagerly.

"If you was a ol' little boy," said Billy, "it wouldn't make no diffunce; I don't want to make yo' ma mad an' Aunt Minerva say for me to keep 'way f'om you anyhow, though I didn't make her no promises."

Jimmy grew angry.

"You're the stingiest Peter they is, William Hill," he cried; "won't let nobody tech your old mumps. My cousin in Memphis's got the measles; you just wait till I get 'em."

Billy eyed him critically.

"If you was ol' —" he was beginning.

Jimmy thought he saw signs of his yielding.

"And I'll give you my china egg, too," he quickly proposed.

"Well, jest one tech," agreed Billy; "an' I ain't a-goin' to be 'sponsible neither," and he poked out a swollen jaw for Jimmy to touch.

Ikey Rosenstein at this moment was spied

by the two little boys as he was walking
jauntily by the gate.

"You better keep 'way f'om here, Goose-
Grease," Jimmy yelled at him; "you better
get on the other side the street. Billy here's
got the mumps an' he lemme tech 'em so's
I can get 'em, so's my papa and mama'll
lemme do just perzactly like I want to; but
you're a Jew and Jews ain't got no business
to have the mumps, so you better get 'way.
I paid Billy 'bout a million dollars' worth to
lemme tech his mumps," he said proudly.
"Get 'way; you can't have 'em."

Ikey had promptly stopped at the gate.

"What'll you take, Billy, to lemme get
'em?" he asked, his commercial spirit at once
aroused.

"What'll you gimme?" asked he of the
salable commodity, with an eye to a bargain.

Ikey pulled out a piece of twine and a blue
glass bead from his pocket and offered them

to the child with the mumps. These received
a contemptuous rejection.

"You can do perzactly like you please
when you get the mumps," insinuated Jim-

my, who had seemingly allied himself with
Billy as a partner in business; "grown folks
bound to do what little boys want 'em to
when you got the mumps."

Ikey increased his bid by the stub of a

lead pencil, but it was not until he had parted with his most cherished pocket possessions that he was at last allowed to place a gentle finger on the protuberant cheek.

Two little girls with their baby-buggies were seen approaching.

"G' 'way from here, Frances, you and Lina," howled Jimmy. "Don't you come in here; me and Billy's got the mumps and you all 'r' little girls and ought n' to have 'em. Don't you come near us; they're ketching."

The two little girls immediately opened the gate, crossed the yard, and stood in front of Billy. They inspected him with admiration; he bore their critical survey with affected unconcern and indifference, as befitted one who had attained such prominence.

"Don't tech 'em," he commanded, waving them off as he leaned gracefully against the fence.

"I teched 'em," boasted the younger boy. "What'll you all give us if we'll let you put your finger on 'em?"

"I ain't a-goin' to charge little girls nothin'," said the gallant Billy, as he proffered his swollen jowl to each in turn.

A little darkey riding a big black horse was galloping by; Jimmy hailed and halted him.

"You better go fast," he shrieked. "Me and Billy and Frances and Lina's got the mumps and you ain't got no business to have 'em 'cause you're a nigger, and you better take your horse to the lib'ry stable 'cause he might ketch 'em too."

The negro boy dismounted and hitched his horse to the fence. "I gotter little tarrapim—" he began insinuatingly.

And thus it came to pass that there was an epidemic of mumps in the little town of Covington, and William Green Hill grew rich in marbles, in tops, in strings, in toads, in chewing gum, and in many other things which comprise the pocket treasures of little boys.

CHAPTER XXIII

THE INFANT MIND SHOOTS

MISS MINERVA had bought a book for Billy entitled "Stories of Great and Good Men," which she frequently read to him for his education and improvement. These stories related the principal events in the lives of the heroes but never mentioned any names, always asking at the end, "Can you tell me who this man was?"

Her nephew heard the stories so often that he had some expression or incident by which he could identify each, without paying very much attention while she was reading.

He and his aunt had just settled themselves on the porch for a reading.

Jimmy was on his own porch cutting up

funny capers, and making faces for the other child's amusement.

"Lemme go over to Jimmy's, Aunt Minerva," pleaded her nephew, "an' you can read to me to-night. I'd a heap ruther not hear you read right now. It'll make my belly ache."

Miss Minerva looked at him severely.

"William," she enjoined, "don't you want to be a smart man when you grow up?"

"Yes'm," he replied, without much enthusiasm. "Well, jes' lemme ask Jimmy to come over here an' set on the other sider you whils' you read. He ain't never hear 'bout them tales, an' I s'pec' he'd like to come."

"Very well," replied his flattered and gratified relative, "call him over."

Billy went to the fence, where he signaled Jimmy to meet him.

"Aunt Minerva say you come over an'

listen to her read some er the pretties' tales you ever hear," he said, as if conferring a great favor.

"Naw, sirree-bob!" was the impolite response across the fence, "them 'bout the measliest tales they is. I'll come if she'll read my Uncle Remus book."

"Please come on," begged Billy, dropping the patronizing manner that he had assumed, in hope of inducing his chum to share his martyrdom. "You know Aunt Minerva'd die in her tracks 'fore she'd read Uncle Remus. You'll like these-here tales 'nother sight better anyway. I'll give you my stoney if you'll come."

"Naw; you ain't going to get me in no such a box as that. If she'd just read seven or eight hours I wouldn't mind; but she'll get you where she wants you and read 'bout a million hours. I know Miss Minerva."

Billy's aunt was growing impatient.

"Come, William," she called. "I am waiting for you."

Jimmy went back to his own porch and
the other boy joined his kinswoman.

"Why wouldn't Jimmy come?" she asked.

"He—he ain't feeling very well," was
the considerate rejoinder.

"Once there was a little boy who was
born in Virginia—" began Miss Minerva..

"Born in a manger," repeated the inat-
tentive little boy to himself; "I knows who
that was." So, this important question settled in his mind, he gave himself up to the
full enjoyment of his chum and to the giving
and receiving of secret signals, the pleasure
of which was decidedly enhanced by the
fear of imminent detection.

"Father, I can not tell a lie; I did it with
my little hatchet," read the thin, monoto-
nous voice at his elbow.

Billy laughed aloud—at that minute

Jimmy was standing on his head waving two chubby feet in the air.

"William," said his aunt reprovingly, peering at him over her spectacles, "I don't see anything to laugh at," — and she did not, but then she was in ignorance of the little conspiracy.

"He was a good and dutiful son and he studied his lessons so well that when he was only seventeen years old he was employed to survey vast tracts of land in Virginia—"

Miss Minerva emphasized every word, hoping thus to impress her nephew. But he was so busy, keeping one eye on her and one on the little boy on the other porch, that he did not have time to use his ears at all and so did not hear one word.

"Leaving his camp fires burning to deceive the enemy, he stole around by a circuitous route, fell upon the British and—"

Billy held up his hands to catch a ball which Jimmy made believe to throw.

Miss Minerva still read on, unconscious of her nephew's inattention:

"The suffering at Valley Forge had been intense during the winter—"

Billy made a pretense behind his aunt's upright back of throwing a ball while the other child held up two fat little hands to receive it. Again he laughed aloud as Jimmy spat on his hands and ground the imaginary ball into his hip.

She looked at him sternly over her glasses:

"What makes you so silly?" she inquired, and without waiting for a reply went on with her reading; she was nearing the close now and she read carefully and deliberately:

"And he was chosen the first president of the United States—"

Billy put his hands to his ears and wriggled his fingers at Jimmy, who promptly returned the compliment.

"He had no children of his own, so he is called the Father of his Country."

Miss Minerva closed the book, turned to the little boy at her side, and asked:

"Who was this great and good man, William?"

"Jesus," was his ready answer, in an appropriately solemn little voice.

"Why, William Green Hill!" she exclaimed in disgust. "What are you thinking of? I don't believe you heard one word that I read."

Billy was puzzled; he was sure she had said "Born in a manger." "I didn't hear her say nothin' 'bout bulrushes," he thought, "so 'tain't Moses; she didn't say 'log cabin,' so 'tain't Ab'aham Lincoln; she didn't say 'Thirty cents look down upon you,' so 'tain't Napolyon. I sho' wish I'd paid 'tention."

"Jesus!" his aunt was saying, "born in Virginia and first president of the United States!"

"George Washin'ton, I aimed to say," triumphantly screamed the little boy, who had received his cue.

CHAPTER XXIV

A FLAW IN THE TITLE

OME on over," invited Jimmy.

"All right; I believe I will," responded Billy, running to the fence. His aunt's peremptory voice arrested his footsteps.

"William, come here!" she called from the porch.

He reluctantly retraced his steps.

"I am going back to the kitchen to bake a cake and I want you to promise me not to leave the yard."

"Lemme jes' go over to Jimmy's a little while," he begged.

"No; you and Jimmy can not be trusted together; you are sure to get into mischief, and his mother and I have decided to keep the fence between you for a while. Now, promise me that you will stay right in my yard."

Billy sullenly gave her the promise and she went back to her baking.

"That's always the way now," he said, meeting his little neighbor at the fence; "ever sence Aunt Minerva got onto this-here promisin' business, I don't have no freedom 't all. It's 'William, promise me this,' an' it's 'William, don't ferget yo' promise now,' tell I's jes' plumb sick 'n' tired of it. She know I ain't goin' back on my word an' she jest nachelly gits the 'vantage of me; she 'bout the hardest 'oman to manage I ever seen sence I's born."

"I can nearly all time make my mama do anything 'most if I jus' keep on trying and keep on a-begging," bragged the other boy; "I just say, 'May I, mama?' and she'll all time say, 'No, go 'way from me and lemme 'lone,' and I just keep on, 'May I, mama?

May I, mama? May I, mama?' and toreckly she'll say, 'Yes, go on and lemme read in peace.'"

"Aunt Minerva won't give in much," said Billy. "When she say 'No, William,' 'tain't no use 'tall to beg her; you jest wastin' yo' breath. When she put her foot down it got to go just like she say; she sho' do like to have her own way better'n any 'oman I ever see."

"She 'bout the mannishest woman they is," agreed Jimmy. "She got you under her thumb, Billy. I don' see what womans 're made fo' if you can't beg 'em into things. I wouldn't let no old spunky Miss Minerva get the best of me that way. Come on."

"Naw, I can't come," was the gloomy reply; "if she'd jest tol' me not to, I coulder went but she made me promise, an' I ain't never goin' back on my word. You come over to see me."

"I çan't," came the answer across the fence; "I'm earning me a baseball mask. I done already earnt me a mitt. My mama don't never make me promise her nothing; she just pays me to be good. That's huccome I'm 'bout to get 'ligion and go to the mourner's bench. She's gone up town now and if I don't go outside the yard while she's gone, she's going to gimme a baseball mask. You got a ball what you bringed from the plantation, and I'll have a bat and mitt and mask and we can play ball some. Come on over just a little while; you ain't earning you nothing like what I'm doing."

"Naw; I promis' her not to an' I ain't ever goin' to break my promise."

"Well, then, Mr. Promiser," said Jimmy, "go get your ball and we'll throw 'cross the fence. I can't find mine."

Billy kept his few toys and playthings in a closet, which was full of old plunder. As he reached for his ball something fell at his feet from a shelf above. He picked it up, and ran excitedly into the yard.

"Look, Jimmy," he yelled, "here's a baseball mask I found in the closet."

Jimmy, forgetful of the fact that he was to be paid for staying at home, immediately rolled over the fence and ran eagerly toward his friend. They examined the article in question with great care.

"It looks perzackly like a mask," announced Jimmy after a thorough inspection, "and yet it don't." He tried it on. "It don't seem to fit your face right," he said.

Sarah Jane was bearing down upon them. "Come back home dis minute, Jimmy!" she shrieked, "want to ketch some mo' contagwous 'seases, don't yuh? What dat y' all got now?" As she drew nearer a smile of recognition and appreciation overspread her big good-natured face. Then she burst into

a loud, derisive laugh. "What y' all gwine
to do wid Miss Minerva's old bustle?" she
enquired. "Y' all sho' am de contraritest
chillens in dis here copperation."

"Bustle?" echoed Billy. "What's a bustle?"

"Dat-ar's a bustle—dat's what's a bustle. Ladies use to wear 'em 'cause dey so
stylish to make dey dresses stick out in de
back. Come on home, Jimmy, 'fore yuh
ketch de yaller jandis er de epizootics; yo'
ma tol' yuh to stay right at home."

"Well, I'm coming, ain't I?" scowled the
little boy. "Mama needn't to know nothing
'thout you tell."

"Would you take yo' mama's present now,
Jimmy?" asked Billy. "You ain't earnt it."

"Wouldn't you?" asked Jimmy, doubt-
fully.

"Naw, I wouldn't, not 'thout I tol' her."

"Well, I'll tell her I just comed over a

minute to see 'bout Miss Minerva's bustle," he agreed as he again tumbled over the fence.

A little negro boy, followed by a tiny white dog, was passing by Miss Minerva's gate.

Billy promptly flew to the gate and hailed him. Jimmy, looking around to see that Sarah Jane had gone back to the kitchen, as promptly rolled over the fence and joined him.

"Lemme see yo' dog," said the former.

"Ain't he cute?" said the latter.

The little darkey picked up the dog and passed it across the gate.

"I wisht he was mine," said the smaller child, as he took the soft, fluffy little ball in his arms; "what'll you take for him?"

The negro boy had never seen the dog before, but he immediately accepted the ownership thrust upon him and answered without hesitation, "I'll take a dollar for her."

"I ain't got but a nickel. Billy, ain't you got 'nough money to put with my nickel to make a dollar?"

"Naw, I ain't got a red cent."

"I'll tell you what we'll do," suggested

Jimmy; "we'll trade you a baseball mask for him. My mama's going to gimme a new mask 'cause I all time stay at home, so we'll trade you our old one. Go get it, Billy."

Thus commanded Billy ran and picked up the bustle where it lay neglected on the grass, and handed it to the quasi-owner of the puppy. The deal was promptly closed and a black little negro went grinning down the street with Miss Minerva's ancient bustle tied across his face, leaving behind him a curly-haired dog.

"Ain't he sweet?" said Jimmy, hugging the fluffy white ball close to his breast. "We got to name him, Billy."

"Le's name her Peruny Pearline," was the prompt suggestion of the other joint owner.

"He ain't going to be name' nothing at all like that," declared Jimmy; "you all time got to name our dogs the scalawaggest name they is. He's going to be name' 'Sam Lamb' 'cause he's my partner.''

"She's a girl dog," argued Billy, "an' she can't be name' no man's name. If she could I'd call her Major."

"I don't care what sort o' dog he is, girl or boy, he's going to be name' 'Sam Lamb.' Pretty Sam! Pretty Sam!" and he fondly stroked the little animal's soft head.

"Here, Peruny! Here, Peruny!" and Billy tried to snatch her away.

The boys heard a whistle; the dog heard it, too. Springing from the little boys' arms Sam Lamb Peruny Pearline ran under the gate and flew to meet her master, who was looking for her.

CHAPTER XXV

EDUCATION AND ITS PERILS

T was a warm day in early August and the four children were sitting contentedly in the swing. They met almost every afternoon now, but were generally kept under strict surveillance by Miss Minerva.

"'T won't be long 'fore we'll all hafto go to school," remarked Frances, "and I'll be mighty sorry; I wish we didn't ever hafto go to any old school."

"I wisht we knowed how to read an' write when we's born," said Billy. "If I was God I'd make all my babies so's they is already eddicated when they gits born. Reckon if we'd pray ev'y night an' ask God, He'd learn them babies what He's makin' on now how to read an' write?"

"I don' care nothing at all 'bout them babies," put in Jimmy, "'tain't going to do us no good if all the new babies what Doctor Sanford finds can read and write; it'd jes' make 'em the sassiest things ever was. 'Sides, I got plenty things to ask God for 'thout fooling long other folks' brats, and I ain't going to meddle with God's business nohow."

"Did you all hear what Miss Larrimore, who teaches the little children at school, said about us?" asked Lina importantly.

"Naw," they chorused, "what was it?"

"She told the Super'ntendent," was the reply of Lina, pleased with herself and with that big word, "that she would have to have more money next year, for she heard that Lina Hamilton, Frances Black, William Hill, and Jimmy Garner were all coming to school, and she said we were the most notoriously bad children in town."

"She is the spitefullest woman they is,"
Jimmy's black eyes snapped; "she 'bout the
meddlesomest teacher they is in that whole
school."

"Who telled you 'bout it, Lina?" questioned the other little girl.

"The Super'ntendent told his wife and
you know how some ladies are,—they just
can't keep a secret. Now it is just like
burying it to tell mother anything; she
never tells anybody but father, and grandmother, and grandfather, and Uncle Ed, and
Brother Johnson, and she makes them
promise never to breathe it to a living soul.
But the Super'ntendent's wife is different;
she tells ever'thing she hears and now
everybody knows what that teacher said
about us."

"Everybody says she is the crankiest
teacher they is," cried Jimmy. "She won't
let you bring nothing to school 'cepting

your books; you can't even take your sling-shot, nor your air-gun, nor—"

"Nor your dolls," chimed in Frances, "and she won't let you bat your eye, nor say a word, nor cross your legs, nor blow your nose."

"What do she think we's goin' to her ol' school fer if we can't have fun?" asked Billy. "Tabernicle sho' had fun when he went to school. He put a pin in the teacher's chair an' she set down on it plumb up to the head an' he tie the strings together what two nigger gals had their hair wropped with, an' he squoze up a little boy's legs in front of him with a rooster foot tell he squalled out loud, an' he th'owed spitballs, an' he made him some watermelon teeth, an' he paint a chicken light red an' tuck it to the teacher for a dodo, an' he put cotton in his pants 'fore he got licked, an' he drawed the teacher on a slate. That's what you go to

school fer is to have fun, an' I sho' is goin'
to have fun when I goes, an' I ain't goin'
to take no bulldozin' offer her, neither."

"I bet we can squelch her," cried Frances,
vindictively.

"Yes, we'll show her a thing or two," —
for once Jimmy agreed with her; "she 'bout
the butt-in-est old woman they is, and she's
going to find out we 'bout the squelchingest
kids ever she tackle."

"Alfred Gage went to school to her last
year," said Frances, "and he can read and
write."

"Yes," joined in Jimmy, "and he 'bout the
proudest boy they is; all time got to write
his name all over everything."

"You 'member 'bout last Communion
Sunday," went on the little girl, "when they
hand roun' the little envellups and telled all
the folks what was willing to give five dollars more on the pastor's sal'y just to write

his name; so Alfred he so frisky 'cause he
know how to write; so he tooken one of the
little envellups and wroten 'Alfred Gage' on
it; so when his papa find out 'bout it he say
that kid got to work and pay that five dollars
hisself, 'cause he done sign his name to it."

"And if he ain't 'bout the sickest kid they
is," declared Jimmy; "I'll betcher he won't
get fresh no more soon. He telled me the
other day he ain't had a drink of soda water
this summer, 'cause every nickel he gets
got to go to Mr. Pastor's sal'ry; he says he
plumb tired supporting Brother Johnson
and all his family; and, he say, every time
he go up town he sees Johnny Johnson
a-setting on a stool in Baltzer's drug store
just a-swigging milk-shakes; he says he going
to knock him off some day 'cause it's his
nickels that kid's a-spending."

There was a short silence, broken by
Billy, who remarked, apropos of nothing:

"I sho' is glad I don't hafter be a 'oman when I puts on long pants; mens is heap mo' account."

"I wouldn't be a woman for nothing at all," Jimmy fully agreed with him; "they have the pokiest time they is."

"I'm glad I am going to be a young lady when I grow up," Lina declared. "I wouldn't be a gentleman for anything. I'm going to wear pretty clothes and be beautiful and be a belle like mother was, and have lots of lovers kneel at my feet on one knee and play the guitar with the other—"

"How they goin' to play the guitar with they other knee?" asked the practical Billy.

"And sing 'Call Me Thine Own,'" she continued, ignoring his interruption. "Father got on his knees to mother thirty-seven-and-a-half times before she'd say, 'I will.'"

"Looks like he'd 'a' wore his breeches out," said Billy.

"I don't want to be a lady," declared Frances; "they can't ever ride straddle nor climb a tree, and they got to squinch up their waists and toes. I wish I could kiss my elbow right now and turn to a boy."

CHAPTER XXVI

UNCONDITIONAL SURRENDER

HEY'S going to be a big nigger 'scursion to Memphis at 'leven o'clock," said Jimmy as he met the other little boy at the dividing fence; "Sam Lamb's going and most all the niggers they is. Sarah Jane 'lowed she's going, but she ain't got nobody to 'tend to Benny Dick. Wouldn't you like to go, Billy?"

"You can't go 'thout you's a nigger," was the reply; "Sam Lamb say they ain't no white folks 'lowed on this train 'cep'in' the engineer an' conductor."

"Sam Lamb'd take care of us if we could go," continued Jimmy. "Let's slip off and go down to the depot and see the niggers get on. There'll be 'bout a million."

Billy's eyes sparkled with appreciation.

"I sho' wish I could," he said; "but Aunt Minerva'd make me stay in bed a whole week if I went near the railroad."

"My mama'd gimme 'bout a million licks, too, if I projected with a nigger 'scursion; she 'bout the spankingest woman they is. My papa put some burnt cork on his face in the Knights er Pythi's minstrels and I know where we can get some to make us black; you go get Miss Minerva's ink bottle too, that'll help some, and get some matches, and I'll go get the cork and we can go to Sarah Jane's house and make usselfs black."

"I ain't never promise not to black up and go down to the depot," said Billy waveringly. "I promise not to never be no mo' Injun—I—"

"Well, run then," Jimmy interrupted impatiently. "We'll just slip down to the railroad and take a look at the niggers. You don't hafto get on the train just 'cause you down to the depot."

So Miss Minerva's nephew, after tiptoeing into the house for her ink bottle and filling his pockets with contraband matches,

met his chum at the cabin. There, under the critical survey of Benny Dick from his customary place on the floor, they darkened their faces, heads, hands, feet, and legs; then, pulling their caps over their eyes, these energetic little boys stole out of the back gate and fairly flew down an alley to the station. No one noticed them in that hot, perspiring, black crowd. A lively band was playing and the mob of good-humored, happy negroes, dressed in their Sunday best, laughing and joking, pushing and elbowing, made their way to the excursion train standing on the track.

The two excited children got directly behind a broad, pompous negro and slipped on the car just after him. Fortunately they found a seat in the rear of the coach and there they sat unobserved, still and quiet, except for an occasional delighted giggle, till the bell clanged and the train started off.

"We'll see Sam Lamb toreckly," whispered Jimmy, "and he'll take care of us."

The train was made up of seven coaches, which had been taking on negroes at every station up the road as far as Paducah, and it happened that the two little boys did not know a soul in their car.

But when they were nearing Woodstock, a little station not far from Memphis, Sam Lamb, making a tour of the cars, came into their coach and was promptly hailed by the children. When he recognized them, he burst into such a roar of laughter that it caused all the other passengers to turn around in their seats and look curiously in their direction.

"What y' all gwine to do nex' I jes' wonder," he exclaimed. "Yo' ekals ain't made dis side o' 'ternity. Lordee, Lordee," he gazed at them admiringly, "yo' sho' is genoowine, corn-fed, sterlin' silver, all-wool-an'-a-yard-wide, pure leaf, Green-River Lollapaloosas. Does yo' folks know 'bout yer? Lordee! What I axin' sech a fool question fer? Course dey don't. Come on; I gwine to take y' all off 'm dese cars right here at dis Woodstock, an'. we kin ketch de 'commodation back home."

"But, Sam," protested Billy, "we don't want to go back home. We wants to go to Memphis."

"Hit don't matter what y' all wants," was the negro's reply, "y' all gotta git right off. Dis-here 'scursion train don't leave Memphis twell twelve o'clock to-night an' yuh see how slow she am running, and ev'y no 'count nigger on her'll be full o' red eye. An' yo' folks is plumb 'stracted 'bout yer dis minute, I 'low. Come on. She am gittin' ready to stop."

He grabbed the blackened hand of each, pushing Jimmy and pulling Billy, and towed the reluctant little boys through the coach.

"Yuh sho' is sp'iled my fun," he growled as he hustled them across the platform to the waiting-room. "Dis-here's de fus' 'scursion I been on widout Sukey a-taggin' 'long in

five year an' I aimed fo' to roll 'em high;
an' now, 'ca'se o' ketchin' up wid y'all, I
gotta go right back home. Now y'all set
jes' as straight as yer kin set on dis here
bench," he admonished, "whilst I send a tele-
graph to Marse Jeems Garner. An' don'
yuh try to 'lope out on de flatform neider.
Set whar I kin keep my eye skinned on yuh,
yuh little slipp'ry ellum eels. Den I gwine
to come back an' wash yer, so y'all look like
'spectable white folks."

Miss Minerva came out of her front door
looking for Billy at the same time that
Mrs. Garner appeared on her porch.

"William! You William!" called one
woman.

"Jimmee-ee! O Jimmee-ee-ee!" called the
other.

"Have you seen my nephew?" asked the
one.

"No. Have you seen anything of Jimmy?" was the reply of the other.

"They were talking together at the fence about an hour ago," said Billy's aunt. "Possibly they are down at the livery stable with Sam Lamb; I'll 'phone and find out."

"And I'll ring up Mrs. Black and Mrs. Hamilton. They may have gone to see Lina or Frances."

In a short time both women appeared on their porches again:

"They have not been to the stable this morning," said Miss Minerva uneasily, "and Sam went to Memphis on the excursion train."

"And they are not with Lina or Frances,"—Mrs. Garner's face wore an anxious look. "I declare I never saw two such children. Still, I don't think we need worry, as it is nearly dinner time, and they never miss their meals, you know."

But the noon hour came and with it no hungry little boys. Then, indeed, did the relatives of the children grow uneasy. The two telephones were kept busy, and Mr. Garner, with several other men on horseback, scoured the village. Not a soul had seen either child.

At three o'clock Miss Minerva, worn with anxiety and on the verge of a collapse, dropped into a chair on her veranda, her faithful Major by her side. He had come to offer help and sympathy as soon as he heard of her distress, and, finding her in such a softened, dependent, and receptive mood, the Major had remained to try to cheer her up.

Mr. and Mrs. Garner were also on the porch, discussing what further steps they could take.

"It is all the fault of that William of yours," snapped one little boy's mother to the other little boy's aunt. "Jimmy is the best child in the world when he is by himself, but he is easily led into mischief."

Miss Minerva's face blazed with indignation.

"William's fault indeed!" she answered back. "There never was a sweeter child than William," for the lonely woman knew the truth at last. At the thought that her little nephew might be hurt, a long-forgotten tenderness stirred her bosom and she realized for the first time how the child had grown into her life.

The telegram came.

"They are all right," shouted Mr. Garner joyously, as he quickly opened and read the yellow missive. "They went on the excursion and Sam Lamb is bringing them home on the accommodation."

As the Major, short, plump, rubicund,

jolly, and Miss Minerva, tall, sallow, angular, solemn, were walking to the station to meet the train that was bringing home the runaways, the elderly lover knew himself to be at last master of the situation.

"The trouble with Billy—" he began, adjusting his steps to Miss Minerva's mincing walk.

"William," she corrected faintly.

"The trouble with *Billy*," repeated her suitor firmly, "is this: you have tried to make a girl out of a healthy, high-spirited boy; you haven't given him the toys and playthings a boy should have; you have not even given the child common love and affection." He was letting himself go, for he knew that she needed the lecture, and, wonderful to tell, she was listening meekly. "You have steeled your heart," he went on, "against Billy and against me. You have about as much idea how to manage a boy as a — as a — " he hesitated for a suitable comparison; he wanted to say "goat," but gallantry forbade; "as any other old maid," he blurted out, realizing as he did so that a woman had rather be called a goat than an old maid any time.

The color mounted to Miss Minerva's face.

"I don't have to be an old maid," she snapped spunkily.

"No; and you are not going to be one any longer," he answered with decision. "I tell you what, Miss Minerva, we are going to make a fine, manly boy out of that nephew of yours."

"We?" she echoed faintly.

"Yes, we! I said we, didn't I?" replied the Major ostentatiously. "The child shall have a pony to ride and everything else that a boy ought to have. He is full of natural animal spirits and has to find some outlet for them; that is the reason he is always in mischief. Now, I think I understand children." He drew himself up proudly. "We shall be married to-morrow," he announced, "that I may assume at once my part of the responsibility of Billy's rearing."

Miss Minerva looked at him in fluttering consternation.

"Oh, no, not to-morrow," she protested; "possibly next year some time."

"To-morrow," reiterated the Major, his white moustache bristling with determination. Having at last asserted himself, he was enjoying the situation immensely and was not going to give way one inch.

"We will be married to-morrow and—"

"Next month," she suggested timidly.

"To-morrow, I tell you!"

"Next week," she answered.

"To-morrow! To-morrow! To-morrow!" cried the Major, happy as a schoolboy.

"Next Sunday night after church," pleaded Miss Minerva.

"No, not next Sunday or Monday or Tuesday. We will be married to-morrow," declared the suddenly dictatorial Confederate veteran.

Billy's aunt succumbed.

"Oh, Joseph," she said, with almost a simper, "you are so masterful."

"How would you like me for an uncle?" Miss Minerva's affianced asked Billy a few minutes later.

"Fine an' dandy," was the answer, as the child wriggled himself out of his aunt's embrace. The enthusiastic reception accorded him, when he got off the train, was almost too much for the little boy. He gazed at the pair in embarrassment. He was for the moment disconcerted and overcome; in place of the expected scoldings and punishment, he was received with caresses and flattering consideration. He could not understand it at all.

The Major put a hand on the little boy's shoulder and smiled a kindly smile into his big, gray, astonished eyes as the happy lover delightedly whispered, "Your Aunt Minerva is going to marry me to-morrow, Billy."

"Pants an' all?" asked William Green Hill.

Printed in the United States
45724LVS00004B/192

9 781417 909681